SUDDENLY IT WENT TO HELL

One of the hardmen in residence emerged from the garage, took one look at Maria with an AK-47 in her hand and froze.

Maria pivoted to face him, squeezing off a burst that punched him backward, flat against the stucco wall. But the lookout on the wall was already shouting the alarm.

Fowler brought the captured rifle to his shoulder, triggering a burst that ripped across his target's legs. He threw himself behind the Bronco's wheel, and Maria scrambled in on the other side.

Fowler twisted the ignition, and he heard the engine fire. He dropped the Bronco into gear, released the parking brake and stood on the accelerator, the fat tires spitting sand and gravel as he took off from a standing start. He found the headlight switch and flicked the high beams on, illuminating three gunners in the glare.

He drove left-handed, the AK-47 braced across his windowsill and spitting lead. He saw one man collapse before he left the targets behind in a drifting cloud of dust.

Then the gate was in front of them, the two gunners braced for action, frozen in the high beams, firing from the hip.

AGENTS

PIPELINE

PAUL MALONE

A GOLD EAGLE BOOK FROM

WORLDWIDE ®

TORONTO • NEW YORK • LONDON • PARIS
AMSTERDAM • STOCKHOLM • HAMBURG
ATHENS • MILAN • TOKYO • SYDNEY

First edition September 1991

ISBN 0-373-63802-7

Special thanks and acknowledgment to
Mike Newton for his contribution to this work.

PIPELINE

PIPELINE

PROLOGUE

When Hector Elizalde struggled back to consciousness, the pain was waiting for him, crouched and ready like a jungle predator, delighted with a brand-new opportunity to make him scream. Instinctively he clenched his teeth and bottled up the sound before it could escape. A flicker of his eyelids was the only sign of life he displayed.

He did not recognize the vehicle, but its uneven rocking motion told him they were driving over rough terrain—the vast and desolate desert.

It was the perfect place to dig a grave.

He spent a moment checking out the damage, tensing arms and legs in turn, discovering no major broken bones. A number of his ribs were cracked, but he could breathe without the jagged, tearing pain that would have meant a punctured lung. His face felt heavy, bloated—fractures there, without a doubt, but nothing that a decent plastic surgeon couldn't fix.

So far, so good.

His hands were cuffed in front of him, his ankles free; an idiot's mistake or smirking gesture of contempt, it did not matter which. The cuffs were tight enough to cut off circulation, numbing everything below his wrists, but Elizalde welcomed the relief from the pain. They had torn his fingernails with pliers, then come back again to snap the digits one by one when he refused to speak.

He made a conscious effort to remember everything, despite the pain those memories awakened in his flesh. How long had they been working on him? Had he broken near the end, when minutes crept along like weeks of screaming agony?

No memory of breaking down, but Elizalde told himself it hardly mattered, anyway. His cover had been blown before they went to work, and nothing he could tell them would have made it any worse.

It was the first time Elizalde had been truly thankful he was working on his own. He had no contacts to betray, as *he* had been betrayed by someone higher up.

He shifted slightly, swallowing the bolt of agony that blasted from his groin, unable to assess the damage there but grateful for his ignorance. His new position eased the rocking of the vehicle a fraction, and the knowledge of betrayal gave him focus, something to distract him from a universe of pain.

Evaluating every move he had made the past ten days, he could not make himself believe he had blown the game. His cover was secure—or *seemed* that way—until the hit team swept him up and took him to the basement, where his interrogators laid out their tools like surgeons scrubbing up for a routine procedure. Nothing out of place, beyond the fact that he was suddenly exposed. As good as dead.

Betrayal.

What began as mere suspicion had become explicit when the leader of the hit team spelled it out.

"Why fight it, Hector? Your *hermano* gave you up. We know you're working for the government. You may as well admit it, save yourself some pain."

Brother? Elizalde had no brothers; he had been an only child. The taunting reference could only mean a brother officer. The covert nature of his mission narrowed down the choices, but he had no time to think about it as the pain began, and he was too damned busy screaming to consider who had sold him out.

And now, with only moments left to live, he knew. If only he could find a way to spread the word before he died....

The van was slowing, gravel spitting from beneath the knobby tires, the driver finally satisfied with their location. Elizalde bit his lip against the pain that flared inside him as they shuddered to a stop.

Be strong. Forget the way you feel.

He had one chance, at best, and he could only make it work if he forgot about the pain and let his rage take over, dominating every other sense. It was a fool's bet, even so, but it was all he had.

There was a sound of crunching footsteps on the sand and gravel—at least two men—before they opened up the double doors in back. One of them climbed inside the van and shone a flashlight in his face.

"Wake up, *pendejo*. Time to party."

They slapped Hector two, three times, with force enough to start a distant ringing in his ears.

The battered captive did his best to imitate a coma victim, grudgingly aroused by sudden pain. His swollen eyes screwed up against the light, he moaned and raised his broken hands as if in self-defense.

"Okay, we got him. Help me move this sack of shit."

A second man leaned in and got a grip on one of Hector's ankles, pulling as the other grabbed his hair and shirt, prepared to shove him out the open door. Another heartbeat now, the only chance he might ever have.

It was a matter of coordination, using every bit of speed and strength he possessed, as Hector raised his free leg, kicking out, connecting firmly with the second gunman's nose. He felt the cartilage give way, and a surge of triumph steeled him against the worst of it, his chained arms lashing out against the gunman crouching over him.

If nothing else, the sudden bolt of agony told Hector that his twisted hands were completely dead. The chain caught his assailant in the face and chipped a couple of his teeth, the impact driving him away and backward as he lost his balance, landing on his ass.

And it was now or never.

The lunge for freedom woke up every throbbing nerve in Elizalde's body, and he screamed as much from panic and frustration as the pain itself. Outside the van, he nearly fell and lost it all before he caught himself, while the second gunner struggled to rise, with dark blood smeared across his face, more splotches of it soaking through his shirt.

"I kill you, *maricón*."

But Hector reached him first, with another kick precisely aimed between the gunman's legs. His target doubled over, gagging, and Elizalde brushed past him toward the open darkness of the desert. Overhead, a silver cuticle of moon provided all the light that he would need.

Ten yards. Fifteen. He gave himself the luxury of hope, against all odds.

And then the bullet brought him down.

He thought it was a leg wound, but the pain that racked his body made it difficult to say with any kind of certainty. One moment he was moving and the next a hammer stroke from nowhere knocked him sprawling in the dirt. Experience told Elizalde that he had not simply tripped and fallen on his own.

The gunman was standing over him a moment later, spitting blood and brandishing a pistol in his face.

"You breathing, man? Tha's good. I want you breathing when I light you up."

He had no more strength to fight as fingers tangled in his hair and he was dragged across the desert floor, back toward the van. His second adversary waited there, hunched over, hands on knees, with murder in his eyes.

Beside him, standing in the open doorway of the van, a bright red can of gasoline.

He wriggled, crawling like a wounded lizard as they doused him, knowing he could not escape. The worst of it so far was knowing he had blown his chance to speak the Judas's name aloud and see himself avenged.

The worst, that is, until his first assailant crouched in front of Elizalde, toying with a wooden match.

"You look a little chilly, Hector. It gets cold out here at night, I know. You need a fire to keep you warm."

The match flared in his hand, described a graceful arc...and then the world exploded, taking Hector with it on a one-way trip to hell. He was screaming, trying not to, stripped of choices as the flames began to strip his bones of flesh. He heard the sound of mocking laughter close at hand, still audible despite his screams, the crackling sound of fresh meat on a grill.

And somewhere in the middle of it, anger at the thought that vengeance would be left to other hands.

Ashes to ashes. Dust to dust.

The crescent moon saw everything, unflinching, and it kept the secret to itself.

1

"I hope you're out there, boys and girls."

Jack Fowler did not raise his voice, although the closest member of his audience was thirty yards away, invisible from where he sat. The tiny microphone concealed beneath the broad lapel of his jacket had sufficient power to reach them all . . . provided it was functioning.

And if it wasn't, then what?

Nothing.

They had checked the system out before he left the office, the receivers reading loud and clear. If there was interference now, it had to be a problem he could not control, so there was no point worrying. At least two members of his backup team were covering the meet with visuals, and they would hit the panic button, loud and clear, if anything went wrong.

Of course, by then, it might already be too late.

He checked his confiscated Rolex, shifting slightly in the driver's bucket of the cherry-red Corvette. The car had been some cocaine cowboy's pride and joy a few months back; these days it served as an addition to the motor pool of the Miami DEA. Another piece of federal rolling stock.

Five minutes left and counting. Fowler kept his fingers crossed—the left hand, anyway—his right was busy repositioning the automatic pistol slung beneath his arm. Then he offered up a silent prayer that Baker and his goons would be on time. Or show at all, when it came down to that.

The outfit had been running wild around Miami and environs for the past eight months, hijacking drug consignments, executing mules when they were in the mood. They didn't always bother, driving home the point that they were not really afraid of witnesses. The killing was a form of recreation, serving to enhance their reputation on the street and nullify resistance in advance.

Heading up the six-man gang was Jerry Baker—short for Jeremiah, product of a holy-rolling Pentecostal household in Columbus, Georgia. Razor-strap religion didn't take with Jerry, and he grew up mean, despising everything his parents stood for in the world. He logged his first arrest at age eleven and got his walking papers from an unforgiving father when he turned fifteen. The road led south to sunny beaches, drugs and money, with a two-year stop at Raiford, where he served time on the farm for a felonious assault. A product of the system and the streets, he learned his trade and picked up allies in the joint. At twenty-three he was prime suspect in a minimum of seven drug-related homicides and three times that many robberies from dealers in the free-fire zone of southern Florida.

The outlaw's known accomplices included four ex-cellmates and a teenage slut who drove the backup car on raids when she was not engaged in helping one or more of Baker's boys unwind in bed. No shrinking violet, she was said to have a sure hand with the razor, an assessment bolstered by assault and weapons charges on her juvey rap sheet.

Fowler had no sympathy for mules or dealers who got burned. They paid their money and they took their chances, banking on a jackpot somewhere down the line. When one of them went down, there were a hundred scumbags waiting in the wings to take his place. The problem was that Jerry Baker and his gang were not content to grab a shipment now and then for personal consumption, rubbing out the carrier for fun. Indoctrinated with a twisted version of the profit motive, they immediately turned around and sold their contraband at auction to the highest bidder, so the poison barely took a break before it hit the streets.

Worse yet, the Baker boys—and girl—had agitated matters in Miami to the point that several major cocaine impresarios were on the verge of open war, each trafficker believing one of his competitors employed the gang. A sit-down two months earlier had failed to clear the air, when no one was prepared to buy that the raiders were exactly what they seemed to be: a pack of freelance jackals living by their wits and guns, content to live as outlaws—or a separate law unto themselves—within the underworld.

In fact, they had no ties with any standing drug cartel, beyond the brief negotiations necessary to unload their latest stash. At times they sold to dealers they had robbed a month or two before; some other shipments wound up out of state, unloaded in Atlanta or Mobile. In any case, the predators no sooner had the cash in hand than they were spending freely, working through their loot until they had to plan another score for pocket change.

With a close-knit team like that, no syndicate behind them, infiltration was a hopeless case. Jack Fowler played it out the only way he could, by posing as an up-and-coming dealer on the prowl for any product he could find, regardless of its source. The word got back to Baker in a week or so, and Fowler took a kilo off his hands in a preliminary buy. It was a chance to feel each other out and lay the groundwork for a larger deal, downrange. When Fowler asked for major weight, the cocky con was happy to comply. The previous Tuesday, Baker and his pack had taken down a shipment out of Bogotá, two runners living on machines in ICU and twenty-seven kilos in the wind.

The way it worked, a call got through to Fowler at his cutout number, with a message that the shipment could be his if he came up with thirteen large per key. It beat the going rate by three, four thousand dollars on a kilo, but the Baker gang had little overhead and zero importation costs. The word went back that Jerry's kids had made themselves a deal. Delivery was scheduled on Sunday morning near the amphitheater in Bay Front Park.

The only thing he had to do was wait.

The Caddy Fleetwood showed up ninety seconds later, rolling south on Biscayne Boulevard and braking for the entrance to the parking area. Through its tinted windows, Fowler couldn't get a head count, but he figured Baker riding shotgun, one of his commandos at the wheel and another gun or two in back, for comfort's sake. It would be asking too much for the whole damned crew to turn out on a buy.

"It's show time," he informed the agents staked out at surrounding vantage points. "Stay tuned."

The Fleetwood pulled in nose-to-nose with his Corvette, and Jerry Baker climbed out on the rider's side. He wore a leather aviator's jacket, scruffy by design, to cover up the hardware he habitually carried whenever he left the outfit's hideaway. His driver did not budge, but kept the engine running. Fowler never had a prayer of scoping out the troops.

He took the simulated gator briefcase with him, holding it left-handed as he stepped out of the car.

"We're on," he said to Baker, jiggling the case for emphasis, "as soon as I can taste the goods."

"You don't mind if I make a count?" The outlaw's voice was soft, low-pitched. He could have been a crooner, under different circumstances.

"Not at all."

He passed the case to Baker and watched him place it on the Fleetwood's fender to open the lid. There were deep rows of hundred-dollar bills inside, all confiscated under asset seizures in the past six months. The hijack artist bent forward, his head almost inside the case, as if he could not see six inches from his nose.

"I really love the way it smells," Baker said, grinning like a hungry reptile. "Money. Nothing like it in the fucking world."

"My taste?"

"We got a little problem, there," the outlaw told him, fastening the latches on the case, not taking it in hand.

"What kind of problem?" Fowler asked.

"I got another offer on the load. A better deal, in fact. I couldn't very well say no to sixteen large a kilo."

"What the hell—"

"But, then again, I didn't want to stand you up. It's rude, you know? I hate rude people worse than anything."

"You sold the shit?"

"All gone."

"And now, you're burning me," Fowler said, making sure they got it on tape.

"It sucks, I know . . . but hey, that's life."

"You want to think again."

"I thought enough, already."

Baker was pulling back the right side of his jacket before he finished speaking, revealing a compact Ingram submachine gun hanging underneath his armpit on a swivel mount. Jack was crouching, edging backward as he got a hand inside his coat and found the automatic waiting there.

Before he had a chance to fire, his adversary staggered, slumped against the Fleetwood's fender, toppling the briefcase from its perch. A fist-size crimson flower blossomed on his chest above the heart, and he was halfway to the ground before Jack heard the echo of a rifle shot somewhere behind him, to the left.

His cover weighing in, without a second left to spare.

And Baker's door was standing open when the wheel-man put it in reverse and powered out of there, with rubber biting asphalt, laying trails of sound and smoke. Beyond the Caddy, on the far side of the parking lot, Jack Fowler saw his backup closing, some of them on foot, a federal four-door rolling out to close the exit tight.

They recognized the nature of the trap as Fowler came erect, his automatic steady in a firm, two-handed grip. No points, if he were to be graded on the basis of a classic Weaver stance, but he could move this way. He advanced on the Caddy as it backed away, with nowhere much to go.

The driver lost it midway through a fair one-eighty, Baker's door still flapping like a broken wing. Jack saw the driver, blond hair spilling over naked shoulders in a skimpy halter top, a look of unadulterated venom on her young-old face. The Fleetwood's bumper clipped an old VW minibus, and the impact shook her up enough to make her stall the engine, grinding on it, pedal on the floor and flooding it.

The Caddy wasn't going anywhere.

She bailed out, but Fowler had his hands full with a gunner just emerging on the rider's side. Dark hair cut short enough to show his scalp, a lightning-bolt design shaved on the side. His outfit was a denim mix-and-match, prefaded, and the shotgun in his hands had been sawed off to minimize the need for pinpoint marksmanship.

The stubby piece would level three or four men with a single round at twenty feet—if Fowler let him fire. The choice boiled down to no damned choice at all, and Jack squeezed off three shots before his enemy could swing the 12-gauge pump around. One of them missed and drilled the window post beside his target, but the other two went home, a shoulder and a chest wound bouncing him against the car. He lost the shotgun, going down, and lay immobile where he fell.

Inside the Cadillac, his partner had some kind of automatic weapon and was laying down an aimless burst to cover his retreat. Jack did not have a shot, his target bolting on the other side, the car between them like a shield. He let the others handle it, advancing cautiously until he knelt beside the gunner he had shot, bent down and skimmed the shotgun out of reach.

There was another burst of firing, answered by the double blast of shotguns going off together, close enough that the blasts were almost merged as one. He didn't have to see the gunner fall to know that he was in a world of hurt . . . if he was feeling anything at all.

The skinhead's pulse was weak, fading in and out, but there was still a chance that he could make it if the paramedics didn't stop for doughnuts on their way. He twitched and muttered something incoherent, making faces as he lay there with his cheek pressed flat against the blacktop, oozing life.

The blonde was cursing when they brought her back in handcuffs, kicking out at agents holding her on either side until they dropped her on her face and cuffed her ankles, with a chain between the manacles to keep her legs bent at the knees. It took three men to put her in the car for transport, but they got it done and slammed the door behind her, cutting off the fingernails-on-chalkboard shrieking of her voice.

An ambulance arrived in moments. The attendants wrote off Jerry Baker and the other body before they bundled Fowler's skinhead up and carried him away, their lights and siren forcing traffic to the curb on Biscayne Boulevard.

"Case closed." One of the backups grinned at him, standing over Baker's prostrate body like a big-game hunter with his latest kill.

"Not quite. We've still got two at large."

"They won't get far. You cut the head off any snake, the body dies."

"Be careful where you sit. A dead snake might just bite you in the ass."

"What's eating you?"

Fair question, Fowler thought, and he was reaching for an answer when another voice distracted him. Ed Croson, leader of the second backup team, was approaching in a hurry on his flank.

"Hey, Jack, you got an urgent on the two-way. Stano wants you in the coop, ASAP. He says he'll square your leaving early with the shooting team."

"Right now?"

"Immediately, if not sooner."

Fowler swore softly under his breath.

It was against procedure for an agent to depart a shooting scene without debriefing, casualties excepted, and he knew the rumble must be something else for his control to set the rules asides.

More trouble, right. As if the past few minutes weren't enough to make his day.

"Hey, check the bright side," Croson offered. "Maybe some old fart you never heard of croaked and left you megabucks."

"With my luck," said Fowler, "all he'd leave me is the funeral tab."

"Eternal optimism. That's my boy."

"So, what the hell. You ever see a silver lining didn't have a cloud attached?"

"Not lately."

"There you go."

2

The federal building in Miami stood on Flagler Street, a mile due east of Biscayne Bay and Bay Front Park. It occupied a corner lot and filled up half a block from north to south, a high rise housing agents of the FBI and IRS, probation officers and the United States attorney's office, federal marshals, Health and Human Services, along with various recruiters for the Army, Air Force, Navy and Marines. The southeast corner of the seventh floor was occupied by Florida division offices of the Drug Enforcement Administration, covering activities of ten resident offices throughout the state.

An urgent call from Rudy Stano had to be bad news. He did not run his office like some other law enforcement brass, where *everything* was an emergency and agents knew their top priority was covering the boss's ass. He would not hit the panic button for a missing box of paper clips or last week's tabloid editorial about the need to legalize cocaine. A rumble out of Stano's office—on a Sunday, yet—meant some unknown problem had to be resolved posthaste, and flying blind set Fowler's teeth on edge.

It took him most of half an hour to complete the trip, with morning traffic. Fowler had no competition in the underground garage, and in a quick five minutes he'd locked up his car and was waiting for the elevator to arrive. On seven, he was greeted by eerie silence in place of normal office sounds, reminding Fowler of a scene

from some low-budget flick about the aftermath of
World War Three.

He found the door to Rudy's office standing open, no
one home, a cup of coffee cooling on the desk. Instead
of walking in and acting as though he owned the place,
he doubled back and checked for Stano in the squad
room. He found a rookie agent named Hernandez by his
lonesome, pulling Sunday duty on the phones.

"You seen the man?"

"He's in and out," Hernandez answered. "If he isn't
in his office, you could try the john."

"No thanks, I'll wait."

"Some heavy action at the park, I guess?"

"We pulled it out."

"I wish I could've been there, man. Four months, I'm
lucky if I get to escort prisoners to court."

"You'll get there," Fowler told him, sounding like a
promise. He tried to remember if he'd ever felt that
young and eager on the job.

"I hope so, man."

"Don't push. You're looking for the action, it'll find
you soon enough."

"You think?"

"This time next year, you'll wish you still had Sun-
days on the phone."

Hernandez grinned and shook his head. "No way."

"Hey, Jack?"

The sound of Rudy Stano's voice brought Fowler's
head around. His supervisor was in shirtsleeves, a stocky
five-ten, his collar open and his tie pulled down, a snubby
Colt revolver on his hip. The weapon made his pants sag
slightly on the right, but it was always there at need. And
Fowler knew from personal experience that it was not for
show.

He left Hernandez to his solitary vigil and trailed Stano back along the hall. He was a bit surprised when Rudy closed the office door behind him, circling around the desk to take a seat and waving Fowler toward the only other chair.

"What's up?"

Stano answered with a question of his own. "You got this Baker thing wrapped up?"

"Not quite. A couple of his shooters still at large, but we've got feelers out."

"We'll let the B team clean it up. I've got a little something different you should look at now you've got the time."

Jack nodded, waiting, knowing that he did not need to push. Stano was a twenty-year veteran of federal narcotics enforcement who cut his teeth on the classic "French connection" bust in New York City, making the shift when DEA supplanted the Bureau of Narcotics and Dangerous Drugs in 1973. The years showed in his face, and the sandy hair was shot through with gray, but there was steel and muscle underneath.

"You never worked in Mexico."

It did not come out sounding like a question. Fowler took a chance and answered anyway.

"Not yet."

"I don't suppose you ever met an agent by the name of Hector Elizalde?"

Fowler thought about it, reaching back for names from the academy at Quantico. "It doesn't ring a bell."

"He would've come in after you, I guess. A six-year man. He worked in Texas, out of the McAllen district office."

Past tense. Fowler felt his hackles rising, but he kept the feeling to himself.

"The Hispanic background, he did lots of work across the border. In and out around Laredo, Ciudad Juarez, like that. He had a look-in on that Matamoros deal, a couple years ago. The voodoo thing, remember?"

"Sure."

It wasn't all that easy to forget the video displays of mutilated corpses lifted from a common grave, dilapidated ranch house in the background. Thirteen people that they knew of, sacrificed by psycho dealers to a list of gods who were supposed to make the dopers bullet-proof. As things worked out, it didn't take.

"Okay, long story short," said Stano, getting to the point. "A couple weeks ago, the *federales* took a call about a body someone found outside Guerrero. That's some dinky border town near Laredo, fifty miles or something. Anyway, the guy was toast. It took 'em all this time to make an ID from his teeth, and I suppose we're lucky they even tried."

"It's Elizalde?"

Stano nodded. "Houston sent a whiz kid down from their forensic lab, and he confirmed it. There was evidence of torture, or at least a beating prior to death. Some ribs were broken, all his fingers, hairline fractures of the facial bones and skull."

Jack didn't want to ask, but he could not resist. "The cause of death?"

"Some asshole torched him. Gasoline, they're pretty sure from gas chromatographs. The scarring on his throat and lungs confirm he was alive and breathing when they lighted him up."

"Any cooperation from the law down there?"

"Don't hold your breath. Some kind of pissant marshals in the little towns. Outside the major urban centers, *federales* run the show. You know what that means, when it comes to helping out the DEA.''

Jack knew, indeed. The average police salary in Mexico peaked around $2,400 per year, and *mordida*—institutionalized bribery—was the grease that kept things moving from the border to the presidential palace in Mexico City. In 1985, embarrassed by police involvement in the murder of a DEA undercover agent, Mexican officials grudgingly confessed discovery of ''substantial criminal links between narcotics traffickers and police agents in Mexico.'' The brains behind that murder, as it happened, was a ranking officer in Mexico's Federal Security Directorate, one Tomás Morlet. Jailed for several days pending investigation of murder charges, he was soon released by *federale* comrades on the grounds of ''insufficient evidence.'' Humiliated by the ''cruel injustice'' he had suffered, Morlet angrily resigned his federal post and moved to voodoo-ridden Matamoros. There, within a year, he was acclaimed the most successful smuggler of narcotics in the state of Tamaulipas, acting free of any interference or harassment by police.

In short, and with some readily identifiable exceptions to the rule, *los federales* played a dirty game of politics and profits. They were Johnny-on-the-spot with clubs and guns whenever college students staged a demonstration or a group of peasant workers tried to organize a union for themselves, interrogating ''rebels'' with cattle prod or six-pack up the nose, but they were worse than useless when it came to busting big-time drug cartels. The few who did not have their hands out, quickly learned to think of blindness as a form of life insurance, while the rest jumped in the cesspool with their boots on, sometimes doubling up as hit men for the syndicates when they ran short of triggermen.

"So far," said Rudy, "all we've got from Mexico is the ID on Elizalde and the cause of death. First they said it could have been an accident while he was camping. Set himself on fire while he was toasting a burrito, I don't know. They had to let that slide when no one found a campsite, and the medic out of Houston showed them evidence of beating prior to death."

"They didn't like that much, I guess."

His supervisor shrugged. "Mañana land down there, you know. They take everything in stride. If Elizalde was a U.S. agent operating in the sovereign state of Mexico without cooperation from the duly deputized authorities...blah, blah. You know the song and dance by now."

"It's Elizalde's fault that he got killed."

"Hell, yes. When all else fails, you blame the victim for a while, buy time to think it through. Before too long we ought to be expecting charges that he sold his mission out and started moving drugs himself."

"A possibility?"

"We're looking at it, just to cover all the bases. I don't know this kid from Adam. One or two of his superiors out there I recognize on sight, but that's about the size of it. I couldn't tell you whether he was clean or not. Right now, it doesn't matter either way."

"How's that?"

"I got a call last night from Grady Sears, division chief in Houston. We go back a ways together. Anyhow, he's worried that there might be dirt around the office, but he isn't thinking Elizalde."

"A leak, for instance?"

"More or less."

"You think some douche bag in the structure sold him out deliberately."

"Unless the poor guy fucked himself somehow. I wouldn't rule it out, but everything I'm hearing says he was a classic pro. He hated drugs from checking out the junkies in the barrio while he was growing up. Suspended from his high school twice for roughing up the campus dealers, this and that."

"Hey, even good guys make mistakes."

"Of course. That's why we're double-checking every aspect of the case to run down any loose ends that were overlooked before."

"Who's *we?*"

"Sears doesn't want to put his people on the touchy stuff until he's sure about their loyalty. We've worked it out to trade four agents, straight across. McAllen gets a wire man, plus a couple of interrogators."

"Me?"

"It's strictly voluntary, Jack. You walk away, I find somebody else and no hard feelings. Okay?"

"Let's hear what he was working on."

A momentary silence hung between them, with Fowler waiting while Stano shuffled papers on his desk and opened a thick manila folder to hand Jack a sheaf of glossy photographs.

"On top, you're looking at Miguel Ignacio Reynoso, rated number one among the dealers in Chihuahua. Once upon a time he was a street kid, like they all start out, in some little town halfway between the Rio Grande and nowhere. After this and that, he put some cash together, bought himself a poppy field or two. Expanded into marijuana when he started making money. These days he'll move anything that sells. The money's in cocaine."

"He's not a tunnel rat, by any chance?"

"No confirmation, but if someone told me Reynoso had a piece of that, I wouldn't be surprised."

Some months before, a team of DEA investigators had unearthed a tunnel, several hundred feet in length, which ran beneath the border from Nogales, Mexico, into Nogales, Arizona. Stripped of useful evidence but plainly operational for several years at least, the subterranean approach had been a new twist on the border-crossing game. Nobody had a clue how many tons of stuff had passed along that tunnel, headed north; how many wetbacks and illegal weapons it had carried to *El Norte* while crates and satchels full of greenbacks flowed back the other way.

Nobody knew how many other tunnels might be operating on the border, even now.

"Your Spanish holding up?" asked Stano.

"Sí."

"That's cute. I'm glad you've kept your sense of humor, Jack."

"Some days it feels a little strained."

"I told you this was strictly volunteer, and that's the truth. You buy a piece of it, we plan to put you on the ground in Ciudad Juarez, an open sore across the border from Laredo. Place makes Tijuana look like a religious theme park. Anything you want—and I mean *anything*—you come up with the scratch in Ciudad Juarez, it's yours."

"What am I looking for?"

"A new connection for your salesmen on the street. Some heavy pharmaceuticals to cut the slack, before those conscientious DEA commandos smoke you out of house and home. Top dollar for an introduction to Reynoso and a look inside, before you cut a deal."

It had the makings of a classic sting, but there were built-in problems he could not ignore. "Who knows about this trade-off at the Texas end?"

"Well, Sears. A couple of his people in administration, I suppose."

"You'll want to check them out before we're in too deep."

"I'm way ahead of you. It's in the works."

"Nobody we can absolutely trust, across the line?"

"The cops are anybody's guess. You might get lucky, but I wouldn't hold my breath. The way it looks to me, you're on your own."

"And if it sours . . ."

"We'd have to go through channels, right. The embassy is highly sensitized to drug enforcement problems at the moment, so a phone call or a drop-in ought to get results."

That was assuming he had access to a vehicle or telephone, of course, assuming he was still alive to call or drop in at the embassy.

"I'll make a note."

"We're touching up a cover now, in case you bought it. Details will be in your hands today by five o'clock."

Jack had a troubling thought. "This wasn't Elizalde's gig, by any chance?"

"No way." The graying supervisor looked insulted by the very notion. "He was running wets across the border for a while, before they started letting him move packages. It was the slow way round, but it was worth a shot. He never made it past Reynoso's middlemen."

"If all else fails . . ."

"Try knocking on the front door, right. It's worked a time or two before, if I recall."

"I hate to be predictable."

"One gripe I've never had during the time we've been together." Sobering, Stano added, "If I didn't think you had a decent shot, I'd let Sears take the job and shove it up his ass."

"You know him pretty well, I take it?"

"Grady? We came up together, working in the Bronx and Queens. Those days you had to speak Italian, eat spaghetti on the stakeouts till you had it coming out your ears."

"Tough job."

"It had its moments. Anyway, we're talking Grady Sears. He saved my life one night when a couple of the wise guys thought they could make their bones a little quicker with a Fed."

"Times change."

"Men, too. I hear you. If I thought there was a chance that Grady sold his own man out and got him fried that way, I'd pull the fucking plug myself."

"Okay."

"You want it?"

"No," he answered honestly. "But what the hell?"

3

The sprawling complex of apartments filled a city block due east of Shenandoah Park. It was your basic stucco anthill, overpriced and short on maintenance, but Jackson Fowler called it home. His numbered "private" parking space was empty, a surprise event that happened once or twice a year, most commonly around the holidays. He filled it, smelling residue of gun smoke on his hands and clothing as he cranked the window up and checked around the seats, made certain nothing vital would be left behind.

Instead of taking the direct route to his three-room walk-up, Fowler circled wide around the complex, homing in on the rental office and the bank of mailboxes in front. His box gave up two bills, a travel magazine, a flyer marked Urgent and cleverly addressed to Occupant. Some outfit called the Prison Ministry was asking him to put a con through college. Fowler dropped it in the round file on his way back home.

Apartment living was about the best a single Fed could manage in Miami, short of going on the pad, and Fowler liked to sleep at night, on those occasions when he got the chance. His car was two years old but looked like new, a product of the bodywork required to fill in bullet holes and straighten fenders from a job-related incident three months ago. If it survived the next two years, it would be Fowler's, free and clear.

He had considered moving out some weeks before, when heavies from a pending case had found out where he lived. They weren't a problem any more—three dead and one upstate at Raiford, doing twenty-five to life—and Fowler had decided it wasn't worth the aggravation, running every time trouble showed up at his door. Five years with Metro-Dade and nine with DEA had taught him one eternal truth: When shit comes down, there's nowhere anyone can hide.

The shift from Metro-Dade Narcotics to a federal badge nine years ago had been a move to put his life on track and keep it there. It wasn't that the payoffs tempted Fowler—stepping up to DEA had only made the opportunities for graft that much more lucrative—but he was sick and tired of getting nowhere on a job that should have been a breeze.

In Fowler's view, a cop's assignment was simplicity itself. You ran down human predators and took them off the street, case closed. He understood the Bill of Rights and countless technicalities involved, accepting all of it with the assumption he could still find ways to do his job.

Strike one.

In point of fact, the courts and high-priced lawyers had a great deal less to do with slowing Fowler down than members of his own department. Some cops had their hands out, scooping up whatever they could steal and actively obstructing justice in the process. Others were consumed with office politics, intent on scoring brownie points and undermining any competition for promotion somewhere down the line. A few had been around so long their attitudes were petrified, a herd of dinosaurs in uniform. The net result was chaos in the ranks, with major cases thrown away—deliberately or otherwise—with good cops forced to make their own way on the streets, occasionally cutting corners as they tried to do their jobs.

The DEA meant starting out from scratch, with thirteen weeks at Quantico designed to weed out any shrinking violets in the class. At twenty-nine, Jack Fowler was a year beyond the average age for new recruits, and several members of his class were bright-eyed youngsters fresh from college, armed with nothing but their bachelor of arts degrees. One applicant in every hundred is accepted for the DEA academy, and nine percent of those wash out ahead of graduation day, but Fowler stayed the course. Nine years and too much violence later, he had no sincere regrets about his choice.

Of course a federal badge was not the cure for every problem he had faced at Metro-Dade. Bureaucracies around the world share many common traits, regardless of their labels, and it didn't help that orders sometimes had to find their way from Washington instead of city hall. Jack knew that raiders intercepted less than ten percent of the narcotics smuggled into the United States, and he was painfully aware that leaders of the Medellín cartel would bank at least three billion dollars in the next twelve months alone.

Still, they were making progress, kicking ass and taking names. Some thirty-five percent of federal prisoners from coast to coast were serving time on cases generated by the DEA. In asset forfeitures, Miami led the nation easily, two hundred million dollars' worth of cash and other items confiscated from narcotics dealers in the latest fiscal year. If blood was spilled and lives were lost along the way...well, progress always had its price.

It was a start, at least. The first step on a long and bloody road, with no end yet in sight.

A rookie agent, starting fresh, usually came into DEA expecting relocation to a city far from home, but Fowler's prior experience around Miami led the brass to leave him there, where he had contacts on the city force and snitches on the street. It was an opportunity for him to pay some debts, resolve a few old scores, and for the most part he had used it well. He knew the game in southern Florida as only veteran players can, and he was bent on coming out ahead.

But the side trip into Texas and across the border was a different matter entirely.

It was a temporary measure, granted—in and out, with any luck at all—but temporary sometimes had a way of going terminal when there were drugs and guns involved. The talk about a new face on the scene was just another way of saying he would be a stranger, stuck on unfamiliar turf, with no one he could trust. One agent was dead already, and his automatic urge for payback did not camouflage the built-in dangers waiting for him.

His fluency in Spanish was a plus, but on the flip side, he was just another gringo once he crossed the Rio Grande. If Hector Elizalde had not pulled it off—much less if he had been betrayed by someone on his own home team—the odds against success for Fowler would be even worse. He put the numbers out of his mind deliberately and concentrated on the job at hand.

Connecting with a dealer in a town like Ciudad Juarez should be no sweat. By all accounts, narcotics were the city's covert stock-in-trade, with buyers from El Paso dropping over for a taste, importers from as far away as Brooklyn, Montreal and San Francisco bearing cash to keep the local scum in military hardware, silk and limousines. Reynoso was a cut above the rest, a prince among the peasants, but he would not be unreachable.

It all depended on the proper bait.

Across the board, narcotics dealers lived on greed and kept themselves alive with paranoia, weeding out com-

petitors and enemies by any means available. The best—
or worst—of them were brutal avarice personified, disguising fear with arrogance, adept practitioners of the
preemptive strike.

But it was always business first.

Without a steady flow of drugs and cash, no dealer
could afford the guns and muscle necessary for his own
survival. In a murky world where violence and decep-
tion were the rule, successful traffickers were forced to
seek expanding markets for their poison, picking up new
customers and outlets day by day. New trade meant
strangers, wild cards in the deck, and any dealer could be
reached if you were slick enough to pass the entrance test.

The cover was of prime importance.

With Rudy Stano's help, he would become John
Decker, late of the Atlanta federal penitentiary, where he
had served the first half of a five-year jolt for importation of cocaine. The real John Decker was a fading
memory, last heard from in the neighborhood of Carta-
gena, when he tried to stiff a pair of heavy hitters for the
price of seven keys. But he survived on paper, in the files
at Metro-Date and DEA, the federal prison system and
the FBI. If anybody ran it back, they would discover
thirteen felony arrests with two convictions, all on drug-
related counts.

So far, so good.

It would have been a crap shoot, using Decker's name
around Miami, but the odds against encountering an old
acquaintance in the northern states of Mexico were slim
to none. His mug shots had been pulled on Rudy Stano's
order two weeks after Decker's murder was confirmed,
so that his jacket could be used for an occasion such as
this. In time, if Fowler had not used the name, some

other federal agent would have tried it on for size. They might again some day, in any case.

For now, as far as anyone in Texas or Chihuahua was concerned, Jack Fowler *was* John Decker. If they picked him off, then it would be the first case Fowler knew of where a dealer bit the big one twice.

It was a crazy twist on being born again, but Fowler was accustomed to the changing names and manufactured histories employed when he was working under cover. Sometimes, when an agent went too deep or stayed too long, the line between reality and make-believe was blurred, or disappeared completely. Some got lost along the way, forgetting who they were and what they were supposed to do. Temptations of the flesh, from easy cash to easy women, jarred some agents off the track, and they could never find their way back home.

In Fowler's case, there was no crisis of identity. He knew the bad guys going in, and they were always in his sights. The problem was they were expert hunters in their own right, capable of smelling danger in the wind. Surrounded by an entourage of gunmen and attorneys, dirty cops and politicians, they could kill long-distance, well before a solitary tracker got in range to make his shot.

On paper it was simple. Find a contact on the streets of Ciudad Juarez and put the word out he was looking for a major source. Sit back and wait for cautious nibbles from Reynoso's outfit, someone on the fringe at first— a pilot fish to check him out. Explain the kind of weight and money he had in mind, insisting on a parlay with the man in charge to fix a deal. No middlemen or second-stringers need apply.

It was a tried-and-true approach, dependent for success upon an agent's cover...and his nerve. The most authentic paperwork available would be no help disguising fear, anxiety, self-doubt. An agent working under cover had to walk a tightrope every waking hour of the day and even in his sleep. The surest way to blow a sting was acting nervous when he should be cool, or coming off too casual when any normal dealer would be wired. There was no safety net to catch him if he fell.

In normal circumstances, working stings around Miami, there would always be the fallback option of a call to Rudy Stano for some backup. Find a telephone, and he could whistle up a SWAT team anytime he needed, request a meeting or a wiretap on his subject's line. If Fowler needed earnest money for a buy, more hardware—damn near anything at all—he had it at his fingertips.

No more.

Once he set foot in Mexico, it was a different game. He had no legal jurisdiction there, and some of the authorities were known to act as spies and muscle for the opposition. Fowler would be on his own, without a helping hand if he got turned around somehow and lost his way.

So be it.

Rudy Stano would be doing half of Fowler's packing for the trip. An Oyster suitcase, scuffed to match his own, chock-full of hundred-dollar bills. One hundred C-notes in a bundle, and one hundred bundles to the case. A million reasons why Reynoso ought to meet this gringo, one-on-one, and find out what was on his mind.

The second case held Fowler's clothes and toiletries, his shoulder holster and a sleek Beretta 92-F automatic pistol, recently adopted by the U.S. military to replace the venerable Colt .45. His standard-issue Glock was registered in Washington, and therefore it was traceable if he was killed or captured by the enemy. For this trip he was flying sterile, nothing but his face and fingerprints to give him up, if it came down to that.

The automatic would be safe enough when Fowler checked his luggage at the Miami airport, but he could not afford to show his federal badge and wear a firearm on the plane. Instead he would be carrying a special five-inch knife, initially designed for agents of the CIA assigned to foreign service. Molded from a blend of fiberglass and nylon, it was sharp enough to slit a throat and tough enough to penetrate a half-inch slab of plywood, all without the risk of setting off security devices geared for weapons with metallic parts.

He had no reason to expect a hassle on the flight, but with a risk of leaks in Texas, it was possible someone would be waiting for him on the other end. If so, and they proved hostile, he would have a fighting chance at any range within arm's length.

No blinking light indicated a message on his answering machine. Grateful for small favors, Fowler got himself a beer from the refrigerator, sat and thought about Reynoso, fifteen hundred miles away. With Elizalde's cover blown, he had to know the DEA was breathing down his neck, but that was status quo for dealers in the Mexican's position, heading up a major network on the Tex-Mex border. Fowler's task would be to slip inside his guard and do it now, before Reynoso's paranoia had an opportunity to level off after finding one Fed close to home.

No easy job, but Fowler wasn't being paid to stroll around the park and wait for heavies to surrender on their own. He had to build a case and make it stick if they were going to dismantle the Reynoso dope machine.

He swept the coffee table clean and laid out copies of the photographs supplied by Rudy Stano. Focusing on

Reynoso's smiling face, he saw no humor in the eyes. His dark hair was immaculately styled, his profile clean and sharp—a classic Hispanic.

Number two in the Reynoso network was Jesús Lopez Dominguez, the resemblance to his namesake ending with the dark hair worn at shoulder length, most often tied back in a ponytail. His partial rap sheet, garbled in translation, listed twenty-three arrests since age fifteen, including two for homicide that didn't stick. Not bad for eight years' time.

The other shots were aerials of the Reynoso spread, midway between Chihuahua and the free-fire zone of Ciudad Juarez. It was a long walk to the border from his rancho, sunbaked buttes and desert all the way, with rattlesnakes and scorpions for company. The overflight gave Fowler an impression of the layout's size, its isolation, with a narrow dirt road in and out, a helipad in easy walking distance of the house.

The place was designed for quick getaways, while anyone who tried to storm the compound found himself exposed, with the defenders granted interlocking fields of fire. An airlift could be used to leapfrog gunners on the wall, but raiders coming in by plane or helicopter would be spotted miles from target by the radar dish positioned near Reynoso's tennis court.

The only surefire way inside was a Reynoso invitation, Fowler's target in the days ahead. A face-to-face and guided tour of the grounds might put him on the track of Hector Elizalde's killers . . . or at least provide sufficient evidence to build a solid extradition case against his host. He could not count on any help from Mexican authorities, but Rudy Stano had a million dollars riding on the play.

And every one of those ten thousand nonsequential numbers had been cataloged and recorded in computer data banks to chart the flow of cash from Ciudad Juarez to various Reynoso allies in America. If Fowler made his touch, there would be extra heat along the border in the next few days.

But first he had to get inside and live to talk about it afterward. If he was made, at any point along the way, Reynoso would be smart enough to ditch the cash because it was found money that would cost him nothing when he struck the match.

He thought about the coaching each and every agent of the DEA received before they were approved for undercover work. Prioritize objectives. Itemize the risks involved and maximize security precautions. Recognize the point of no return and let it go if there was no substantial prospect of success.

Audacity was half the battle in a major sting. The other half was caution, knowing when to hang it up and walk away.

Sheer audacity had never been Jack Fowler's problem. Giving up was something else again, a bitter pill he swallowed seldom and with visible reluctance. In the past, his willingness to push a case beyond the danger point had earned him several commendations—when it worked—and reprimands when something went awry.

The dead man in Chihuahua was a stranger, but they shared a common sense of duty, and perhaps, in the long run, a common destiny. Jack Fowler did not count himself a superstitious man, but he shared every working cop's intrinsic fatalism when it came to facing death. The hard part had been picking up a badge and gun the first time. After that, a lawman knew he was spinning out his days on borrowed time.

Examining the snapshots of Reynoso's spread, Jack knew he might be looking at the last place he would ever see on earth. Beyond a normal case of pregame nerves, the knowledge neither frightened nor excited him.

The risk came with the job, and he had willingly accepted both.

Reynoso, on the other hand, was big enough and rich enough these days to cherish marginal illusions of his own security. He was not superman, by any means, but he had cash enough to build himself a palace in the desert, guns and troops enough to weather out a siege. He would expect an army to confront him when his moment came at last.

And therein lay the dealer's weakness.

He would not allow himself to fear a single man. Not yet, when he had just removed one traitor from the fold.

With just a little bit of luck, Reynoso's blind spot would be adequate to land his ass in prison.

It might even get him killed.

4

The noonday sun was waiting for him like a crafty enemy when Fowler hit the sidewalk at the El Paso airport. His flight had been on time, but his departure from the terminal was delayed by some confusion with his reservation for a rental car. When it was squared away, he had the Pontiac Grand Prix paid up for seven days, in Decker's name, and signed for the insurance that would let him walk away scot-free in case of mishaps on the road.

He found the car and stowed his Oyster luggage in the trunk, the cash and automatic pistol undisturbed. A search on leaving the United States was so unlikely it defied all odds, but Fowler was not taking any chances. He had done the necessary paperwork to get himself a tourist card, required for journeys into the interior, and he would play it straight until he crossed the Rio Grande.

He made the exit onto Airport Road, the Fort Bliss Military Reservation on his right, and picked up Highway 62 westbound. A quick run past the zoo and coliseum, veering south before the highway turned into Paisano Drive. He chose the free bridge out of principle and waited while a team of bored inspectors quizzed each motorist in turn, requesting information on their travel plans and verifying mandatory paperwork. In fifteen minutes he was clear and motoring across the river that had never stopped an army—or a load of contraband—from moving north or south.

It had to be imagination, Fowler thought, but there was no denying it felt hotter on the streets of Ciudad Juarez than in El Paso. Sunbaked sidewalks teemed with gringo tourists stopping over for the day in search of merchandise or entertainment they were legally denied at home. The shops and market stalls he passed were long on turquoise, hammered silver, fireworks, pottery and leather goods, but veteran shoppers knew enough to ask around for switchblades, women, drugs, directions to the local donkey show. A fair proportion of the daylight visitors were married-looking couples, some of them with kids in tow, but that would change toward sundown when the streets put on a different face.

He found the Miramar Hotel without a hitch, a block due west of Guadalupe Mission, sheltered from the teeming crush of downtown Ciudad Juarez but close enough for Jack to make the scene on foot. His room was ready, and a teenage bellboy took his luggage, grinning fit to burst when Fowler tipped ten pesos—somewhere in the neighborhood of eighty cents, American.

He had a fair view of the city from his balcony, but it was hot outside, and Fowler left the windows shut. He turned the thermostat as low as it would go, expecting no new Ice Age, and considered what to do about his bags.

In other circumstances, Fowler would have placed his money in the hotel safe, but the amount was sure to raise some eyebrows, and he wanted to control the leaks from this point on. His mission—Decker's mission—would be common knowledge on the street within a few short hours, but he wanted to direct the early rumors on his own, without a reference to specific sums of cash on hand.

Effectively deprived of options, Fowler left the million-dollar suitcase in his closet, then unpacked his clothes before he shed the sweaty outfit he had worn that morning out of Miami. In Jockey shorts and socks, he sat down on the bed and field stripped the Beretta one more time to satisfy himself that it would function on demand.

That done, he finished undressing and headed for the bathroom, cool tile beneath his feet. The shower had a shelf inside for sitting down and different settings on the nozzle for massage or simple spray. He spent a moment on the temperature, accepting tepid in the place of cool, before he stepped inside. The soap was lightly scented, and he lathered twice to cleanse himself of lingering smells from the flight and drive.

Refreshed, he saw no need to start his search immediately, when the average time for dining out in Mexico was nine or ten o'clock. Content to stretch out naked on the bed and let the air-conditioning raise goose bumps, he left instructions for a wake-up call at eight and fell asleep with the Beretta underneath his pillow, one hand wrapped around the pistol's grip.

His luck was holding out. He did not dream.

THE MIRAMAR HOTEL was justly famous for its restaurant, and Fowler lingered over seafood enchiladas with *rellenos* on the side, then emerged into semidarkness on the stroke of ten-fifteen. Beyond the facing row of modern office buildings and competing hostelries the skyline seemed to be on fire, a ruddy glow of neon from the strip joints and cantinas where nocturnal tourists congregated.

A short five-minute stroll brought Fowler to the *avenida,* bodies crushed together on the sidewalk, flashy cars with license plates from Texas, Oklahoma and New Mexico competing with a fleet of battered taxis on their native turf. The tourists were predominantly male, with a sprinkling of young women clinging to their dates and looking badly out of place. Police in rumpled khaki circulated through the press halfheartedly, content to stand and watch unless the action turned to fighting, and only intervening if blood was spilled.

Unlike their working sisters in *El Norte,* prostitutes in Ciudad Juarez were not a fixture on the streets. Instead they worked as "hostesses" in countless dingy bars, or passed their time in brothels where the taxi drivers earned a buck a head for every patron they delivered. Carrying the Latin macho culture to its logical conclusion, hustlers on the street were always male, a motley crew of pimps and pushers, strip-show barkers, wastrels hiding pornographic pictures underneath the army-surplus jackets they wore year-round. Within a block, Jack Fowler had been offered marijuana, reds, a crate of U.S. Army hand grenades, and kinky sex with a reputed virgin in her teens. The hawkers ranged in age from ten or twelve years old to roughly sixty-five.

You did not need a narco dog to smell the grass they smoked along the *avenida.* It was everywhere, competing with the car exhaust and tinny noise pollution spilling out of open doorways, mixed up into chaos on the street. If the police were interested, it didn't show.

Another block and Fowler picked out a taxi driver at random, then climbed in the back, relieved that a defective dome light spared him from examining the vehicle's interior. The cabbie was a slender man, with greasy hair grazing his collar, long face decorated by a pencil-thin mustache.

"Where to, *señor?*"

"I'm looking for a nightclub with some class, *comprende?*"

"Sí." The driver's grin was crooked, showing gold beside a gap in front. "I know the place."

"No dives, amigo. I'm prepared to pay for quality."

"Of course, *señor. Muchachas muy bonitas, sí?* Tequila straight, no water like the burro piss some places sell. Okay?"

"I'm sold."

They drove around the block to put some extra mileage on the meter, crossed the *avenida* going east, and covered something like a quarter of a mile before the cab pulled over, idling at the curb. The nightclub could have passed for any one of several dozen Jack had seen so far, with neon cactus flowers splashed across its stucco face. A painted sign above the doorway, splashed by floodlights, told him he was looking at El Scorpion.

"That's it?"

"No finer club in Ciudad Juarez, *señor.*"

He shrugged and paid the fare, with another twenty in hand for the driver as he stood beside the idling cab.

"I'm interested in making friends," he said. "Especially men who deal in medical supplies, large quantities. *Comprende?*"

"Sí, señor."

"If anybody's interested, the name's John Decker. I'll be staying at the Miramar Hotel."

"Juan Degger. At the Miramar."

"That's close enough."

"Gracias, señor."

"De nada, Slick."

The taxi pulled away, and Fowler stepped inside the smoky club. Three hostesses were poised just inside the threshold, trained to wait their turns. The first in line approached Fowler as his eyes adjusted to the dark. Dark hair worn long across her shoulders, with a straining halter top that barely held her breasts in check, a leather mini reaching around mid-thigh. A model's legs, accentuated by the patent leather spikes that passed for shoes.

"You wish a table, yes?"

"Sure thing."

She took his hand and led him through a fog bank seemingly composed in equal parts of marijuana and tobacco smoke. At a tiny stage at one end of the room a naked woman did calisthenics under spotlights, keeping time to records while the band took five. Their table was a ringside seat, where Fowler had a chance to count her pubic hairs.

The hostess pulled her chair up close beside him, hip to hip, and a warm hand settled on his thigh. Onstage, the woman-child—perhaps eighteen—was playing with her nipples, eyes half closed, hips rolling as she simulated ecstasy. A bruise the shape of Idaho was visible on one round buttock as she made a lazy turn and shook her behind in Fowler's face.

"You like?"

"She's not my type."

The hand inched upward. "Am I your type?"

"Could be."

"First time you come to Ciudad Juarez?"

"That's right."

"Good thing you find me here, first time."

"My lucky day."

She smiled and let her fingers do the walking, home at last. The waitress brought their drinks, and Fowler took a sip. If the tequila wasn't watered, they couldn't be growing cactus like they used to anymore.

The hostess threw her drink back like a pro, left-handed, while her right was busy in his lap.

"The truth is, I'm in town on business."

"Not for fun?"

"Fun is my business."

"Just like me."

"You're getting warm."

"You come upstairs, I show you *hot*."

"Let's talk a while."

"*¿Por que?*"

"I'm looking for a man. We haven't met, but we have things in common, business-wise. You follow me?"

"A business man."

"That's it. His name's Reynoso. Ring a bell?"

He caught a flicker in her eyes, but she was good at covering. Her shrug was calculated to distract him with the contents of her halter top. Instead of falling for it, Fowler palmed a fifty-dollar bill and tucked it in her ample cleavage, leaving Grant some room to breathe.

"That's yours. I've got another one just like it, if you know where I can find the man I'm looking for."

"It's hard," she said, and for a moment Fowler didn't know if she was speaking of Reynoso or his response beneath her hand. "I'm not so good with names, you know?"

"Just do your best."

He finished the tequila, rose and left her there, confused. He shot a backward glance before he reached the exit and saw a tub of lard who had to be the manager standing over her, demanding explanation of the patron's swift departure. Fowler waited long enough to catch the fat man's eye before he let the door swing shut behind him, cutting off the smoke and sound.

Two down and five or six more contacts ought to do the trick. The word would circulate through Ciudad Juarez like ripples in a stagnant pond until they reached Reynoso's ears.

From there, he knew it would be anybody's game.

ANOTHER NINETY MINUTES on the street, and he'd spoken to three more cabbies, half a dozen hostess-hookers, and the surly bouncer at a strip-joint where the "live sex show" turned out to be a grainy copy of *Behind the Green Door,* flanked by naked dancers wriggling lethargically around the giant-screen TV. Six hundred dollars in the wind, including drinks, and it would be a bargain if the contacts helped him find his man.

The last stop on his downtown circuit was a freebie. It was quieter, less prosperous than other dives where he had dropped Reynoso's name. He sat alone and ordered bottled beer to erase the taste of watered-down tequila from his palate. Satisfied with one, he paid the tab and started back toward his hotel.

It is a fact of life that while the desert bakes by day, its temperature begins to plummet once the sun goes down. The lack of vegetation and humidity is part of the equation, nothing in the way of balmy nights that made South Florida a magnet for the geriatric set. The city would not lose as much of its diurnal heat as would the open countryside, but Fowler was relieved that he had worn a jacket, after all. It served a double purpose now, to hide the automatic underneath his arm and keep him warm.

The night clerk at the Miramar put on a smile and shook his head when Fowler asked if there were any messages. He had not counted on a hit this soon, but Fowler acted on the premise that his every move was being scrutinized, reported to his enemies. That way he ran no risk of letting down his guard. It was in keeping with his role as an eager businessman, and when the answer came back negative, he kept it casual, a simple shrug before he walked away.

He rode the elevator up and paused outside his door to check the half-inch bits of thread inserted at the upper right-hand corner and beside the lock. Both undisturbed. It was an ancient trick but still effective; even if a prowler saw the threads, once they had fallen, a precise replacement was improbable.

He used his key and double-locked the door behind him, turning on the compact television for some company. A peeling sticker listed half a dozen channels, but the bulk of them were off the air. His options narrowed down to late news from El Paso and a Spanish-language movie featuring some burly wrestlers and a walking mummy who resembled Andy Warhol. Fowler left the mummy on, the volume low, and wondered why the wrestlers in Mexico were always masked.

A knocking on the door surprised him as he was about to take his jacket off. He reconsidered, one hand covering the grip of his Beretta as he answered.

"*¿Sí?*"

"Federal Judicial Police."

He frowned, backed off, unlocked the door. Four men in matching khaki uniforms, the *comandante* cultivating a mustache, his muscle younger, hard around the eyes. All four packed heavy automatic pistols on their hips, in holsters of the sort the U.S. military favored during World War II.

"John Decker?"

"Right."

The *comandante* moved past Fowler, troops in tow, prepared to make himself at home. Jack left the door conspicuously open and turned to follow the intruders with his eyes. In theory these men were his allies, but they did not know he was DEA, and Fowler could not trust them—not in a system where *mordida* was the rule.

"You have a tourist card?"

"Right here."

He passed it over, waiting while the officer in charge examined it, then slipped it into his own breast pocket. Fowler took a chance.

"I'll need that back."

"In time. You come from Florida?"

"Miami, yeah."

"On business?"

"My vacation."

As they spoke, the troops were poking into Fowler's drawers and checking out his empty suitcase. One of them retrieved the second Oyster from the closet and dropped it on the bed.

"In Mexico, *señor,* deceiving the police is an offense against the law."

"Do tell."

"Attempting to procure narcotics is a felony."

"That's good to know."

"The suitcase. Open it."

"You have a warrant?" Fowler asked.

"Remember where you are, *señor.*"

He nodded, did as he was told and saw the lower-ranking *federales* glancing back and forth at one another as the C-note bundles were revealed. At a gesture from his *comandante,* the nearest trooper stuck a gun in Fowler's face. Another frisked him, coming up with the Beretta and a pair of extra magazines.

"You always carry so much money on a vacation?"

Fowler shrugged. "I like to be prepared."

"It is my duty to arrest you for suspicion of narcotics trafficking."

"I want a lawyer, prior to any questioning."

The *comandante* smiled and stepped in close, his rancid breath in Fowler's nostrils.

"What you want, *señor,* is no concern of mine."

5

The telephone woke Rudy Stano at precisely 3:14 a.m. His eyes came into focus on the digital alarm clock. Immediately wide awake and knowing it was trouble, he groped for the receiver, found it and cut the third ring short.

"Hello?"

"It's Fairchild, Chief."

"You'd better have a reason, Arthur."

"We've got action on the Decker jacket, sir. You asked to be informed, regardless of the time."

"That's right." A cold fist clenching in his gut. "What's happening?"

"Official query out of Ciudad Juarez. Their federal branch. A *comandante* named del Cabo queried Metro-Dade and Justice for a rundown on our man."

"Is he in custody?"

"They didn't say. Just background, for the moment. Wants and warrants, rap sheet, stuff like that. At least we know he's in the game."

Or *was,* thought Stano, but cut off the morbid image in a flash.

"It's holding up?"

"So far, so good. The FBI kicked back the basic information. Metro-Dade was more or less a me-too operation, one or two particulars on Johnny D's connections in Colombia."

"No flag to DEA?"

"Not yet. They know he fell on smuggling charges. My guess is that's all they need to hear, whichever way it goes."

"All right. If there's a callback, keep me posted. Otherwise I'll see you at the usual time."

"Ten-four."

Whichever way it goes.

As Stano knew too well, there were at least three possibilities. If Fowler had aroused the curiosity of honest *federales,* they might pick him up for questioning or send him back across the border with a warning not to show his face again in Ciudad Juarez. If dirty cops were picking up his vibes, the game split fifty-fifty; either Decker's jacket proved his bona fides and cleared the way for Jack to meet Reynoso, or they blew it, and he wound up in a ditch somewhere.

Unable to recapture sleep, he threw the covers back and made his way through darkness to the kitchen. There was no one to protest his raiding the refrigerator, since his wife walked out three years ago. Sometimes, he thought, you never really know a person till they take a hike.

Two-thirty in Chihuahua, and he pictured Fowler in a holding cell, complete with dripping water like the dungeon from an old-time Karloff movie. Fairchild didn't know if Jack had been arrested, or the *comandante* out of Ciudad Juarez was merely fishing, and there wasn't any way for Stano to inquire without a risk of selling Fowler out.

Another waiting game.

It was the worst part of his job, this marking time and staring at the walls when he was desperate to be doing something. *Anything,* as long as it meant getting off his ass and taking action. Some of his contemporaries bitched about the courts, the legislature, budgeting and overtime, but if he had to choose the one thing he hated most, it would have been the helpless feeling when an agent was in the field and couldn't be reached, short of throwing in the towel.

If Fowler was in custody, they'd know it soon enough, but there were no guarantees. It depended on the *federales,* whether they were straight or on Reynoso's payroll. If they were bought and paid for, if Reynoso smelled a rat and wanted Jack out of the picture, it would be simple for a prisoner to disappear. A touch-up on the records—if they even bothered logging his arrest—and there was no way anyone could prove "John Decker" had been taken into custody. A few weeks later, when his body surfaced—*if* it surfaced—everyone in Ciudad Juarez would act surprised.

It was always the same old story.

Disgusted with the waiting after only fifteen minutes, feeling acid in his stomach, Stano made a promise to himself. If Fowler bought the farm, he owed the *comandante* something, on the side.

Del Cabo.

Rudy filed the name away for future reference, made a mental note to check the files and see if they had anything to say about a certain *federale* in Chihuahua. He was fishing, but at least it gave his mind a point of focus, something he could think about instead of scarfing Fritos by the handful, staring at the telephone.

Get dressed and go to work, he told himself. He would have hours with the files before the day shift started coming on. It would not hurt for them to find him at his desk when they arrived.

God help the rookie who forgot his paperwork or stepped on Stano's toes today.

God help Jack Fowler down in Ciudad Juarez.

God help them all.

PORFIRIO LUIS DEL CABO scanned his notes once more before he dragged the telephone across his desk and tapped a number out from memory. It crossed his mind that he should have a scrambler on the line, but he was not concerned. His secret files—the set he kept outside his office under lock and key—were good enough insurance for his freedom and his job.

The distant telephone rang twice before a noncommittal voice responded. *"¿Sí?"*

"El Jefe, por favor."

"¿Quién es?"

"Del Cabo."

"Un momento."

Giving out his name entailed some risk if there were wiretaps at the other end, but there had been no adverse repercussions in the past two years. A *comandante* of the FJP was no one to be trifled with, and he would almost certainly be warned in the event of an investigation being launched.

"¿Porfirio, cómo estás?"

He recognized the flat voice of Jesús Dominguez on the line.

"Bien, Jesús. ¿Señor Reynoso?"

"Called away on business. Can I help you, *comandante?"*

Frowning to himself, del Cabo went ahead. Dominguez was Reynoso's eyes and ears, his strong right arm...but that did not make dealing with the weasel any more agreeable.

"We have a gringo here," del Cabo said. "John Decker, from Miami, Florida. He has been asking questions on the street. It seems he wants to met with your *patrón*."

"A spy?"

"We checked him out. According to the FBI, he has a record of arrests for drug-related crimes. Four months ago he was released from federal prison on a charge of dealing in cocaine."

"I never heard of him," Dominguez said, as if that settled everything.

"He has a million dollars in a bag, Jesús."

Dominguez hesitated, thinking fast. "What does he say?"

"Vacation time," del Cabo answered. "Men like this are not accustomed to cooperating with police."

"Perhaps you could persuade him, eh?"

"Of course . . . but if he is legitimate?"

"We find out, either way."

"He may resent interrogation," said the *comandante*. "If he has a million dollars for *El Jefe,* it may not be wise to anger him."

Dominguez snorted. "He complains, I take the money anyway."

"I had in mind the possibility of future deals. Señor Reynoso may not wish to throw such an opportunity away."

Dead silence came from the other end as Dominguez pondered just how Reynoso would react to negligent dismissal of a multimillion-dollar deal. It did not take a rocket scientist to know that any man who cost *El Jefe* several million dollars would be looking at a world of pain.

"We may have been too hasty." He'd said "we," as if del Cabo shared responsibility for what was brewing in his weasel brain. "You have this gringo?"

"*Sí.*"

"The money?"

"Here."

"Where is he staying?"

"At the Miramar."

"I need two hours. Preparations must be made."

"Of course."

"Release him sometime after five o'clock. And let him take the money."

"*Sí.*"

"All of it."

Sudden anger warmed del Cabo's cheeks, but he was wise enough to hold his tongue. Dominguez was a weasel, true enough, but he was also rabid, and he had a lethal bite.

"He'll have it all, don't worry."

"We're agreed, then."

"*Sí, Jesús.*"

"It's Señor Dominguez."

When del Cabo clenched his fist, the yellow pencil he was holding snapped in half. The anger never made it to his voice. "Of course, Señor Dominguez."

"Excellent."

The line went dead, and del Cabo reached out to drop the handset in its cradle like a man who suddenly discovers dog shit on his hands and can't remember how it got there.

One day, if he was fortunate, del Cabo would be privileged to observe Dominguez in his last extremity. When he had pushed too far, too fast, Reynoso would awake and realize that he was dealing with a lunatic, a man unworthy of the wealth and power he possessed. When the day came, the *comandante* hoped he would be called upon to lend a hand on the disposal team.

It was a day worth looking forward to.

For now, however, he would have to follow orders, swallowing his pride in confrontations with Dominguez, playing out the role he had accepted for himself. His federal badge was power, but del Cabo wasn't fool enough to think that he could move against Dominguez while the weasel still enjoyed Reynoso's blessing and protection in Chihuahua.

He would watch and wait, a seasoned hunter on the track of deadly game. If life had taught him nothing else, he knew that perseverance was rewarded, with a little help from luck and circumstance.

And while he waited, he would think of ways to speed the process of degeneration for Dominguez, which he knew to be inevitable.

In the meantime, there was still John Decker of Miami. A *narcotraficante* who could raise a million dollars four months out of federal prison was a man to watch, del Cabo thought. And it was a policeman's job to watch.

It would take two hours for Dominguez to arrive in Ciudad Juarez. Del Cabo did not know exactly what the weasel had in mind, but he would find out for himself.

When Decker left the jail at five o'clock, he would be followed—but discreetly, nothing to alert him or prevent Dominguez from approaching him at will. If there was trouble on the way, the *comandante* would be warned about it in advance, with ample time to save himself...and guard Reynoso's interest, too.

They also serve who only loiter in the shadows, looking on.

WITHOUT HIS WATCH, which had been removed as a potential weapon on arrival at the station house, Jack

Fowler had to estimate the hours he had been in custody. There were no windows in the small interrogation room to show him whether it was light outside, but hours had elapsed, and his fatigue told Fowler it was creeping up on dawn.

Thus far he had been treated with as much respect as any gringo two-time loser could expect. The *federales* had not beaten him, or poured a six-pack of their favorite carbonated beverage up his nose to make him talk. At first the questions were relentless and repetitive but poorly organized, implicit threats unrealized. He got the feeling that the men in charge of grilling him were merely marking time, and for the past two hours or so he had been left alone.

The waiting made it worse, allowing Fowler's own imagination to unwind. He mentally reviewed the details of his cover story, attempting to discover weak points, any chink that would reveal his true identity or cast his alias in doubt. The *federales* did not have to find out who he was; if they were on Reynoso's pad, just knowing who he *wasn't* would be ample cause to make him disappear.

The cover held, no matter how he turned it inside out or upside down. To break it they would need a friend of Decker's, someone who had knowledge of his murder in Colombia.

Unless they tapped a link at DEA.

Who had the information on the Texas end? The section chief, of course, but even Grady Sears hadn't been told his name or physical description. Working blind was safer than involving strangers, where a leak to the opposing camp was probable. It meant that Fowler could not count on any help from Texas, but on the flip side, it would be more difficult for someone on the pad to sell him out.

More difficult, but not impossible.

He understood that Sears would not be working in a vacuum up in Houston. No man ran a DEA division on his own, which meant that there were various subordinates and secretaries in the picture, any one of them presumably equipped to rifle files, tap into private conversations, sift germs of information from the daily give-and-take. It would require a daily polygraph on every member of the Houston staff to shut off potential leaks...and even lie detectors were mistaken one time out of four.

If a deliberate leak had been responsible for Hector Elizalde's death, the source would be expecting a traditional reaction. A flying squad from the headquarters Office of Inspections perhaps, or headhunters from the Office of Security Programs. An agent's death predictably resulted in all manner of reviews and hearings, lesser business put on hold until the boys from Washington discovered how their man had bought the farm, and why. A dirty member of the staff would not expect another covert move against Reynoso's syndicate this soon, with Elizalde's funeral still a day away. If logic ruled, the culprit would be digging in and covering his ass, prepared to weather out the storm.

Surprise and secrecy.

Together they had been the major selling points of Rudy Stano's plan. And Fowler thought it still might work, unless he was already blown somehow.

He heard the *comandante* coming from a distance, the dull slap of boot heels on the concrete floor outside his cell. The door was opened, and solemn uniforms surrounded him, the officer in front.

"We have no reason to detain you further at the present time," he said. "The money and your personal effects shall be returned."

"My gun?"

"Will stay with me. A law-abiding tourist has no need of weapons in Chihuahua. If you feel yourself in danger, the police are here to help you, day or night."

"That's comforting."

The *comandante*'s smile was cold and brittle, like a sculpture made of ice. "This way," he ordered.

Fowler rose and fell in step behind him, back along the corridor, with khaki muscle bringing up the rear. A meaty sergeant on the booking desk returned his watch and wallet, keys and pocket change. One of his escorts fetched the suitcase, and the *comandante* waited while Fowler made a rapid count.

"Okay."

"Your signature on the receipt, *señor*."

"Seems fair." He signed the sheet in duplicate and watched both copies disappear.

"You will be driven back to your hotel," the *comandante* said. "I trust we will not be called upon to visit you again."

He picked the Oyster up and flashed the officer a mocking smile.

"It's been a slice."

Outside, they put him in the back seat of a squad car, two men in the front, beyond a window reinforced with stout wire mesh. No handles on the inside of his doors to let a prisoner escape.

It crossed his mind that he was going on a one-way ride to some dry arroyo chosen as his final resting place, but Fowler knew the *comandante* would have kept the million dollars for himself if it was execution time. By giving up the cash, the officer was signaling his own complicity, a pact between Reynoso and the *federales* to facilitate a deal.

And Fowler had no doubt that a percentage of the money in his suitcase would be shared with the arresting officers, once he had cut a deal with the cartel. It was the way things worked in Mexico—and anywhere on earth that drugs had grown into a major industry.

After they arrived at the Miramar, his escorts dropped him off without a word, and Fowler made his way inside. A different clerk was shuffling papers at the registration desk, carefully avoiding Fowler's gaze. He waited for the elevator, rode it up and had his key in hand before he reach the numbered door.

Before he stepped inside, a pungent odor of cigar smoke instantly alerted him to company. The *federales* were not smoking when they busted him, and this was fresh. A slender, well-dressed Mexican stood up to greet him as he stepped across the threshold.

Fowler recognized Jesús Lopez Dominguez from his photographs.

"*Buenas días, Señor Decker.*" He was smiling, open hand extended, seemingly alone. "I think we have some business to discuss."

6

"I don't remember meeting you."

The dealer kept his smile in place. "You asked about Señor Reynoso on the street."

"Are you Reynoso?"

"An associate. Señor Reynoso does not meet with strangers."

"Why should I?"

Dominguez shrugged. "You came to us," he said. "If you have changed your mind, then I will bid you adios."

"Hold on a second." Fowler dropped the suitcase where he stood and used one heel to close the door behind him. "How am I supposed to verify that you're Reynoso's man? For all I know, you could be heat."

"There is no heat in Ciudad Juarez, *señor*."

"Somebody ought to clue the *federales* in on that," he snapped. "I spent the past four hours in a holding cell downtown."

"A crude technique, I grant you . . . but effective."

"Say again?"

"Señor Reynoso owns the *federales* in Chihuahua."

"Meaning *he* called out the uniforms?"

"The order came from me, on his behalf."

"I guess you'd better spell that out."

Dominguez shrugged. "A stranger from *El Norte*, asking questions . . . I was understandably concerned."

"The *federales* put your mind at ease?"

"My curiosity was satisfied."

"A stunt like that won't win you any friends where I come from."

"Are you referring to Miami, or the federal prison in Atlanta?"

"Take your pick."

"We have a business to protect," Dominguez said. "I would expect a man of your experience to understand."

"You seem to know a lot about *my* business," Fowler said.

"The bare essentials. You served time for smuggling contraband—specifically cocaine—and were paroled four months ago."

"Don't tell me you've got rules against associating with ex-cons."

"If anything, the opposite. Your record indicates you rejected offers of immunity and served your time without identifying various associates."

"That's business. If I take a fall, the time's all mine. I don't point fingers, and I don't drop names."

"A man of honor."

"Common sense," said Fowler in reply. "I like to think of it as life insurance."

"So. What brings you to Chihuahua, Señor Decker?"

"First things first. I didn't catch your name."

"Jesús Lopez Dominguez," he said through his smile. "You have heard of me, perhaps?"

Jack shook his head, rewarded by a hint of disappointment in the weasel's eyes. "Can't say I have. Of course, I only heard Reynoso's name around Miami in the past two weeks or so. And *that's* what brings me to Chihuahua."

"Please explain."

"You've seen my sheet," he said. "You know I trade in pharmaceuticals. Word has it that your boss deals quantity *and* quality, at decent rates."

"I'm not aware of any product shortage in Miami at the present time."

"There isn't any," Fowler told him, "but the snowstorm hasn't kept the dealer's price from rising every time you turn around. I figure I can tap a different source and undersell the competition, make myself a decent piece of change."

"Your friends in Bogotá may take exception to the change."

"What friends are those?" asked Fowler. "I keep quiet on the fall and do my time alone, so I figure they can show a little gratitude. Turns out, I hit the street and everybody's got amnesia, like they can't remember who the hell I am. The shit I went through, and I'm unemployed."

"You want revenge?"

"I want to make a living," Fowler said. "If it costs Bogotá some customers, that's fine with me."

"Your late associates may not take kindly to the competition."

"Hey, I figure there's enough to go around. Somebody wants to fuck with me, they just might *be* my late associates."

"You would require assistance?"

"That depends upon the action," he replied. "I've got some friends lined up to help me, if I find a decent source."

"Are they reliable, these friends?"

"They take life seriously."

"So. Perhaps, if you could tell me what you have in mind..."

"That's easy. When I left Miami, they were asking sixteen, eighteen thousand for a kilo, wholesale, off the plane. We're talking ninety-seven pure. If I can shave that price by four, five grand a key, I've got a chance to make some major inroads in the marketplace... and my supplier would receive a fixed percentage of the net."

"How much?"

"I'll save the numbers for the man in charge."

Dominguez stiffened, working overtime to keep his smile in place. "It doesn't work that way," he said.

"You're authorized to cut a deal?"

"I screen potential customers. Señor Reynoso does not have time to spare for everyone who seeks an audience."

"I've got a million reasons why he ought to make the time for me."

"A one-time deal?"

"An introduction," Fowler said. "I mean to go the distance, and I'll need fresh product all the way."

"You have the money here?"

The *federales* would have told him that already, but the guy liked playing games. Jack nodded to the Oyster suitcase standing in the middle of the floor.

"Right here."

"May I?"

He made a show of pondering the question, knowing that Dominguez would have brought more muscle if he had a simple rip-off on his mind.

"Why not?"

He dropped the suitcase on the bed and spun the combination dials, released the catch and let Dominguez see the hundred C-note bundles stacked inside.

"How does an unemployed ex-convict raise this kind of money, four months out of jail?"

"Investors," Fowler told him, lowering the Oyster's lid and latching it. "I've still got contacts in Miami. Just because I lose a round to Bogotá doesn't mean I'm playing dead."

"Your contacts must have faith."

"They've seen me work."

"And there is more where that came from?"

"We cut a deal for product I can move in Florida, the only limit on our future is Reynoso's own imagination."

"He is famous as a man of vision."

"Then we ought to get along."

"Perhaps a meeting would be best."

"Just tell me where and when."

"Señor Reynoso's home away from home," Dominguez said. "Right now."

"How long?"

"The trip?"

"The stay."

"Feel free to pack your things."

He worked in contemplative silence, filling up the second bag. It could have been a simple ruse to get him out of Ciudad Juarez before they took the cash and left him with a bullet in his head, but Fowler did not think Dominguez had the balls to screw Reynoso out of a potential megadeal. If they decided he was shamming, they could always kill him later, and the cash would still be there.

His only weapon at the moment was the CIA commando dagger, hidden in his shaving kit. Jack made a show of checking out the contents, taking inventory as he palmed the plastic knife, securing it in his pocket when Dominguez glanced away.

It did not even out the odds by any means, but he felt better with the weapon close at hand.

"All set."

"May I?"

Fowler stepped between Dominguez and the suitcase full of cash. "I need the exercise."

"Of course."

Downstairs, when Fowler headed for the registration desk, Dominguez caught him by the arm.

"The bill is settled."

"I admire your confidence."

"You came to make a deal. It never crossed my mind that you would spurn Señor Reynoso's invitation."

"So he knows I'm coming?"

"He knows everything."

"That must be helpful, in a pinch."

Outside, a beige Mercedes waited in the pale gray light of dawn, the driver stepping out and circling around to get the door as they emerged from the hotel. Jack waited while his bags were loaded in the trunk—no sleight of hand—and then got in the back, Dominguez close behind.

"You want to tell me where we're going?"

"South," Dominguez said.

"That helps."

"Señor Reynoso likes his privacy."

"Okay. You got a blindfold I can wear?"

The dealer's smile was strained. "That won't be necessary. If *El Jefe* does not trust you . . . well, it makes no difference what you see."

The message came through, loud and clear. Dominguez did not have to hide his tracks, because if "Decker" failed to pass inspection by the man in charge, he wasn't coming back. It might turn out that way in any case, but Fowler was committed now, and he had bet his life upon Reynoso's reputation as a hungry businessman.

They picked up Highway 45 from Ciudad Juarez, southbound past Zaragoza on the Rio Grande. A hundred miles to Villa Ahumada, with the desert stretching out on either side of them as sunlight drove the shadows back. A low mountain range, the Sierra del Nido, was visible in the distance, marching to intercept their track, but the driver had other ideas. A few miles south of Villa Ahumada, he turned off the highway, following a narrow access road.

"I hope your boy knows where he's going."

The smile Dominguez showed him now was more relaxed. "I told you that Señor Reynoso has a taste for privacy. The world does not intrude upon him here."

"I would imagine not."

"You are acquainted with the hazards of our trade. The best defense against attack is visibility. A man who cannot be approached is never taken by surprise."

"And he can deal with any little problems that arise, no badges getting in his way."

"A case in point," Dominguez said. "Last year we had a visitor from New York City. An Italian. He was interested in merchandise, as you are, but his attitude was disrespectful. There were . . . difficulties, shall we say?"

"It happens."

"You must understand our way of life, *señor*. A man is nothing without honor. For a guest to openly insult his host with ultimatums, threats . . . it is intolerable."

"I can see your point."

"*El Jefe* is a patient man, but he has limits. The Italian was a coward. He refused the invitation to a duel. Of course, Señor Reynoso had no choice. The man was set at liberty to make his own way home. Across the desert."

"Let me guess. He wasn't smart enough to take his shoes."

Dominguez smiled. "A careless oversight. His clothing also was forgotten."

"How'd he do?"

"Twelve hours, more or less. The sun is merciless. Without a knowledge of the land, there is no water to be found. He looked for shelter in a cave."

"Bad choice?"

"A colony of diamondbacks had much the same idea."

"That smarts."

"Our spotters found him in the afternoon. He took three hours to die."

"One question, if I may."

"Of course."

"What happened with New York?"

"The problem was explained. They understood. We made a deal."

"Well, there you go. One asshole could have saved himself a long walk in the sun."

"I had a feeling you would understand."

"We haven't got a desert in Miami, so we play the flip side. Any problems that arise, we drown them in the Everglades. I figure, what the hell, the gators have to eat."

"Our business calls for men of strength, determination."

"Brains don't hurt," said Fowler. "When a fellow like your boss can build an empire out of sand, he must have something on the ball."

"The empire built on sand has roots of stone."

"I wouldn't be here otherwise. The problem with Colombians, you hit it on the head. There's no respect. You know a man for years and treat him right, but he doesn't know you when the shit comes down. These guys, they use their friends like toilet paper. Anything goes wrong, you're down the tube."

"Señor Reynoso stands beside his friends. As for his enemies..."

"I like a man who takes care of business, either way it cuts. No bullshit, no excuses. Everybody knows exactly where they stand."

"*Bien*. We understand each other."

And they rode a while in silence, Fowler staring at the desert through his tinted window, picturing the long walk to the border from Reynoso's ranch. Perhaps a hundred miles, as buzzards fly, to reach the Rio Grande; another fifty, give or take, before you hit a village on the Texas side.

Too far.

A man embarking on a walk like that had nothing left to lose. He might as well stand fast and try to beat the odds while he had strength enough to strike a killing blow.

Or better yet, he could manipulate the odds, attempt to throw his enemies off balance. Set the bastards up to take a fall where no one walks away.

Those were his alternatives, but when push came down to shove, he would be lucky if he had the choice. Whichever way it went, he was committed to the game, well past the point of no return.

A dark spot in the distance swiftly took shape as rugged walls, with trees and rooftops visible beyond.

"I trust you will enjoy your stay," Dominguez said.

Fowler allowed himself a slow smile. "I wouldn't be surprised."

7

From the road, Reynoso's spread reminded Fowler of a set from *Fort Apache*. Twelve-foot walls encircled the compound, stretching out of sight on either side of massive wooden gates. A rifleman was waiting for them on the catwalk overhead, with radio in hand. Their driver palmed a CB microphone and muttered something Fowler could not hear. A password, obviously, and it did the trick. The gates were open by the time they got there, and the wheelman never even had to touch his brakes.

Inside it was a different world, with grass and trees, resplendent flower gardens testifying to the fact that water *could* be found in the Chihuahua desert, if you just drilled deep enough. The inner walls were dark with creeping vines.

Reynoso's sprawling ranch house had been laid out in a horseshoe pattern to surround an open courtyard on three sides. Inside the box, a minipark had been constructed with a fountain as the central feature, benches interspersed with trees and shrubbery. Beyond the house, a covered swimming pool and open tennis courts, an empty heliport, garages, housing for the pumps and generator, quarters for the live-in help. A radar dish took over where the human sentry's eyes left off.

"No rude surprises," Fowler said.

"Technology at work. It gives us peace of mind."

"I guess it would, at that."

Between the *federales* and his built-in early-warning system, it would be impossible for outside raiders to surprise Reynoso in his lair. That still left infiltration, if an agent had the skill and nerve to pull it off.

But getting in, Jack knew, was only half the battle. If he blew it now, the DEA was out two agents and a million confiscated dollars, all for nothing, while Reynoso and Dominguez went about their business unopposed. The hard part lay ahead of him, convincing a professional to deal for major weight and walking out again with evidence sufficient to support a case in court. One shaky step along the way, and his attempt to even up the score for Hector Elizalde would become a one-way trek to nowhere, underneath the blazing desert sun.

No thanks.

He had one chance to make it work, and Fowler was determined not to wind up as a box lunch for the buzzards in Chihuahua. If it came down to a killing situation, he would take Dominguez and as many of the others with him as he could.

The weasel's voice cut through his private reverie. "Señor Reynoso should be back tomorrow morning. In the meantime, you are welcome to relax, enjoy yourself, make use of the facilities. Besides the pool and tennis court, we have an air-conditioned gym with all the latest gear."

"It sounds too much like work."

Dominguez nodded, smiling. "I agree. You may take comfort in our stock of vintage wines, the gourmet chef, two hundred channels on the television. Any other creature comforts that you may desire."

"I'd say your boss knows how to live."

"He is an inspiration to us all."

Was there a hint of jealousy behind the words? Jack filed it in his mind for future study, stepping into gruesome heat outside the air-conditioned car. He let the driver fetch his bags, deciding paranoia would be out of place in these surroundings when Dominguez obviously had the wherewithal to take the cash by force whenever he desired.

Respect.

It never ceased to boggle Fowler's mind how pimps and pushers, from the old-line Mafia to modern Hispanic drug czars, set such store on the appearance of propriety. It didn't matter if you earned your daily bread by hooking kids on smack or casting teenage girls for snuff films, if you kissed the ruling honcho's pinky ring and laughed at his dusty jokes.

A "man of honor" might have bloody hands, but he would never go for long without a manicure.

He just had time to break a sweat before they reached the house, a wall of cold air waiting at the threshold, raising goose bumps under Fowler's sticky shirt. Dominguez led him to the second floor, along a silent corridor lined with expensive-looking abstract paintings. Their destination was a suite approximately twice the size of Fowler's lodgings at the Miramar in Ciudad Juarez.

"Nice spread," he told Dominguez, checking out French doors opening on a private balcony, the courtyard green and shady down below. Unless you stepped outside, you might imagine that the shade was cool.

"I trust you will find everything you need. If not—" Dominguez pointed to a button mounted on the wall "—one of the servants will assist you."

"I didn't get much sleep last night," he answered. "What I'd like to do is catch a shower, get in forty winks or so before I have a look around."

"Of course. I'll leave instructions that you should not be disturbed before the dinner hour. Nine o'clock?"

"Suits me."

Dominguez left him with a final plastic smile, and Fowler was alone. Despite the heat he stepped out on the balcony for another look around the courtyard from a new perspective, just to orient himself. He had the lay-out fixed in mind and was retreating from the glare of sunlight when a movement on another balcony, directly opposite, commanded his attention.

Glancing up, he found a woman staring at him, dark eyes boring into his before she turned and disappeared inside her room. No servant, judging by the way she dressed, and Fowler knew Miguel Reynoso was a bache-lor, from the information in his file at DEA. The fact that he was single did not mean he was celibate, however, but the woman might as easily belong to someone else.

Dominguez?

Fowler closed the French doors tightly, shutting out the heat. She did not strike him as a woman who would will-ingly abide a weasel, but you couldn't always tell. Where wealth and power were involved, you met all kinds.

She was a beauty, though, and there was something in her eyes that Fowler could not instantly identify. A hint of desperation? Anger? Fear?

It made little difference.

The lady had her problems; Fowler had his own to deal with, and a lack of concentration could be fatal. Focus-ing upon Reynoso and the hours ahead, he stripped down for the shower and took the CIA commando dagger with him as an afterthought.

No one would ever take him for a Boy Scout, but he knew enough about the facts of life—and sudden death—to keep himself prepared.

THE NEW ARRIVAL was a stranger to Maria Escobar, but she had recognized his type on sight. They turned up periodically, discussed their filthy business with Miguel, and left again within a day or two. Most of them were gringos from *El Norte,* with a rare Colombian or black included for variety. From time to time, when there was trouble, they remained.

By definition, as a business partner of Miguel's, the stranger was her enemy. And yet . . .

With the Italian, she had almost been successful. He was charmed by her appearance, captivated by the skill she demonstrated in his bed, a stolen hour on the afternoon before he was supposed to leave. Still flushed with passion, he had sworn to help her, and Maria knew that he had tried.

Why else would he have been eliminated as he was?

She still recalled the vision of his body lying twisted in the pickup truck, all bloated from exposure to the sun, discolored in erratic patches where the snakebites had produced internal hemorrhage. She remembered, too, how Miguel had examined the pitiful remains and glanced back to catch her at the window, remembered his mocking smile and cruel demands that night when she was summoned to his room.

The first time she had run away—or tried to run away—Maria thought Miguel might have her shot, or maybe do the job himself. Reality was worse. He seemed to love her in his twisted way, regarding her as one of the possessions he had purchased over time to decorate his home. And having chosen her, he would not let her go.

The members of his staff were hopeless, bound up to Miguel with loyalty that consisted of equal parts greed and fear. He paid them well and punished their transgressions with a cold brutality that left Maria feeling sick inside. In her four years of captivity, Miguel had never once raised his voice in anger, but he could maim and kill without remorse. Someday, when he grew tired of her, Maria knew that he would kill her, too.

By then, she thought, her death might come as a relief.

She had considered suicide at one point, but the teachings of the church dissuaded her with images of everlasting torment. Next, she thought of murdering Miguel, an act which would immediately seal her fate, but she reserved the ultimate expression of her loathing for a time when every other hope was dashed beyond recall.

While there was still a chance of getting out, however marginal, she searched for ways to make it work. She pretended she did not hate Miguel with every fiber of her being when he touched her, even when his eyes found hers and she was forced to smile.

Of course, he knew the truth—had to know, unless he was completely mad—but she was willing to accommodate the fiction when she planned her final getaway. If she could not persuade one of the visitors to help her, she would try it on her own. Once more, at least, before she finally surrendered hope.

Maria gave herself six months before she absolutely had to act or lose her mind. It was a testimony to her inner strength that she had managed to survive this long without a breakdown, but there had been mitigating factors in her case. Aside from rare occasions when he punished her for some infraction of his private rules, Miguel had not been a demanding master. Once the novelty of their bizarre relationship wore off, the second year or so, he summoned her to service him no more than two, three times a week, and she was otherwise allowed to rest in peace. His generosity was legendary—diamonds and designer clothing, any toy or bauble her heart desired . . . except for freedom.

Sometimes, when he bought her things, Maria felt more like Reynoso's daughter than his captive concubine.

She would approach the gringo stranger cautiously, alert to any signal that he was prepared to give her up. She knew when men were interested, the silent message in their eyes, but it was something else for one of them to barter with Reynoso for his drugs, and then attempt to steal the one possession he professed to prize above all else.

It had been simple wooing the Italian from New York, but he was arrogant enough to think his Mafia connections would intimidate Miguel and persuade him to release Maria as a kind of bonus on their deal. An egocentric sexist pig, he did not understand Miguel's obsession, or the insult he was offering his host by asking that "the little lady" be allowed to join him in Manhattan. By the time he recognized the gravity of his mistake, it was too late to save himself.

Maria felt no grief for the Italian. He had used her and would certainly have kept on using her until she bored him, had he lived. In death he paid for crimes the law had never found a way of punishing. Her only sadness at his passing hinged upon the fact that he had failed to help her get away.

She hoped the gringo had not been forewarned. It would be so much easier to win him over if he did not know the price of failure in advance. This time, with any luck, a way might be devised for her to slip outside the walls, away from the determined scrutiny of ever-present guards.

And if the gringo would not help her, there were others on the way. A gathering of jackals scheduled for tomorrow. It might be her last, best hope for freedom, if she did it right.

Today, tomorrow at the latest, she would have to try.

The feeling of anticipation was a welcome change. It gave her greater energy for what lay head of her, the tasks she must perform in preparation for escape.

Beginning now.

A VERY YOUNG HOUSEMAN came for Fowler at the stroke of nine o'clock and led him to the formal dining room. Dominguez had arrived before him and was lounging in a massive hand-carved chair that must have been Reynoso's when *El Jefe* was at home. Jack's place was set immediately to the dealer's left, and there were thirteen empty chairs.

"We're all alone?"

"Tonight, at least," Dominguez said. "There may be other guests tomorrow."

"Are you sure I won't be in the way?"

"It's not a problem. They are businessmen, much like yourself, and we have ample room."

"I half expected someone else to join us."

"Oh?"

"A woman, actually. I saw her on the balcony across from mine this afternoon."

Dominguez frowned but said nothing while a butler in a tuxedo delivered salads and poured wine for each of them.

"Maria does not mingle with our visitors. Señor Reynoso is a firm believer in the separation of his work and private life."

"She's private, then?"

"*El Jefe*'s woman."

"I admire his taste."

"If you desire companionship..."

"Let's wait and see if I have anything to celebrate to-morrow."

"As you wish."

"About these other visitors..."

The waiter interrupted them again, and Dominguez continued when empty salad plates had been exchanged for rare prime rib.

"I'm sure Señor Reynoso will be pleased to introduce you, if your interests coincide."

"I didn't mean to pry."

"Of course. The food is to your liking?"

Fowler did not have to fake appreciation of the tender beef. "It's perfect," he replied. "Your boss goes looking for a chef, he gets his money's worth."

"It is the same in every aspect of his life." Dominguez hesitated, weighing how much he should tell this gringo, finally deciding it could do no harm. "Would it surprise you to discover that Señor Reynoso was an orphan on the streets of Hermosillo?"

Fowler thought about it for a moment, then finally shook his head. "A man who grows up hungry learns survival at an early age. He knows that quitters never make the cut. The toughest men I ever knew grew up alone, or else in families where it would have been a blessing if their so-called parents disappeared one day."

"You understand that all of this—" Dominguez spread his hands to indicate the house around them, and the grounds beyond "—means nothing to Miguel." It was the first time he had used Reynoso's given name. "He could forsake all this tomorrow and begin again. It is his strength."

"It's good to know I'm dealing with a man," Jack said. "Too many dealers in the States these days, they made a fortune overnight and never had to prove themselves. First sign of trouble, shrinking violets cut and run."

"And the Colombians?"

"They just don't give a shit, you know? It's like they're loco. Guy I used to deal with, crazy bastard had a hundred shooters on the payroll, and he still did half the wet work by himself. He *liked* it, see? He couldn't stand to let it go, regardless of the risk."

"What happened to him?"

"Oh, he left some fingerprints around one time. Too fucking dumb to wipe the doorknobs, this and that. He rode the lightning up at Raiford, six, eight months ago. A couple of his friends are splitting up that money now. He's history."

"A lesson for us all," Dominguez said.

"Damn straight. You can't control the law, get someone else to stand in front of you and take the heat."

"We have no problem with the law here in Chihuahua."

"Makes it nice."

"A solid operating base is necessary for success."

"That's what I mean to have, we cut ourselves a deal. One solid fucking base of operations." Staring at Dominguez, he added, "What it costs, it costs."

The dealer smiled. "I have no voice in the decision, Señor Decker."

"Make it John, all right? Reynoso leaves you running things while he's away... I can't believe he doesn't trust your judgment. Just a little bit?"

"I offer my opinion when he asks."

"That's what I mean, right there. He drops a question on you, any thinking man would answer in his own best interest, am I right?"

"My interest and Señor Reynoso's are the same."

"And I admire your loyalty," Fowler said. "My point is, if an offer sounds okay to you, if it puts some money in the family account, no reason why a man who helps me close that deal should be forgotten. Am I right?"

Dominguez smiled. "I can't imagine the Colombians deceiving you," he said.

"You live and learn, Jesús. I'm learning all the time."

"To profitable partnerships."

Their glasses clinked in a toast as Fowler grinned.

"I'll drink to that."

8

The smell of breakfast cooking woke Jack Fowler shortly after eight o'clock. He lay still for a moment, one hand wrapped around the plastic dagger underneath his pillow, startled to discover he had slept so well. If he had dreamed, the images were lost, and Fowler let them go.

He rose and showered quickly, dressed himself and had his bed made by the time a houseman brought the breakfast tray. Relieved that he was free to dine alone, he waited while the service was arranged and then dug into grapefruit, *huevos rancheros* and thick slabs of bacon, lightly buttered toast with marmalade, black coffee hot enough to sear his tongue. It was delicious, and he put his thoughts on hold until the food was decently disposed of and his dishes cleared away.

Outside, a team of gardeners went about their never-ending task of keeping up the grounds. Between the daily heat and desert wind, their basic job would always be supplying water to the greenery, but they had done the job so well that hedges needed trimming, rye grass waited to be mowed, and there were even weeds to pull. Jack thought the gardeners might double up as soldiers in emergencies, but at the moment none of them were armed.

Escaping from the complex would be difficult, regardless. Two or three men armed with automatic weapons, carefully positioned on the walls, could easily command the house and courtyard, laying down a screen of fire that would make open movement tantamount to suicide. Nocturnal flight would shave the odds, but Fowler had already noted floodlights mounted at strategic points on the perimeter, on ready standby for emergencies.

He was not planning on a bust-out, but it couldn't hurt to take a closer look around the grounds while he was on his own. Reynoso and his nameless guests might not arrive for hours yet, and Fowler reckoned he could use the exercise.

The servants were about their business, but he did not see Dominguez on his way downstairs. Their talk the night before had been encouraging, but only just; he had not dared to push too far, too fast, for fear of stirring up suspicion in Dominguez and inciting him to blow the whistle when Reynoso finally arrived. If nothing else, the germ of an idea was planted in the dealer's mind, and it would have to be enough for now.

The news of "other visitors" en route had momentarily thrown Fowler off his stride, but now he hoped a larger crowd would help him sell Reynoso on the plan he had in mind. They needed a confirmed exchange of cash for drugs, with the delivery of product made on U.S. soil where agents of the DEA could make the tag. With dope and prisoners in hand, a trace of Fowler's numbered cash would close the circle on Reynoso, with sufficient evidence for an indictment in the States. From that point on, the rest of it was up to diplomats and politicians, playing give-and-take.

Unless they all got sick of waiting and dispatched a team to bring Reynoso back by force.

It would not be the first time rules were bent—or broken—in pursuit of public enemies. It mattered only if the judges or defense attorneys caught you at it and you watched a solid case go up in smoke.

Two years before, he had been tapped to join a RAT assignment—a Recon Arrest Team—linking DEA with members of the U.S. military to achieve specific goals. The night in question, Fowler and another federal narc, with half a dozen Green Berets, had stormed a tiny island west of Cat, in the Bahamas, lifting off a major coke supplier as he waited for a shipment from Colombia. They dropped him off outside a sheriff's station in Fort Lauderdale, where he was tagged and bagged before he had a chance to ditch two kilos of cocaine their frisk had somehow overlooked. His lawyers howled about abduction and entrapment, but the RATs were unidentified, and the defendant's various "character witnesses" were unwilling to come forward in the face of pending charges. When the verdict came back guilty, he went down for thirty-five to fifty years.

Case closed.

It would not be that easy with Reynoso, sitting in his desert fortress with its radar dish, protected by a screen of dirty cops and sentries on the walls. If possible, he would prefer to bait a trap and draw Reynoso out of hiding, playing on the one emotion every dealer shared in common with his fellow slime: compulsive greed.

When dealers fell, they used a wide variety of arguments to justify their trafficking in human misery—religion, politics, concern about "their people"—but in fact it came down to profits, when you stripped the layers of bullshit and exposed the inner workings of their minds. A man or woman turned to selling drugs because it had the highest profit margin in the world, outside of counterfeiting, and the cash filling pockets or numbered bank accounts was absolutely genuine. In this case, money literally grew on trees—or bushes, stalks and vines, depending on the product preferred.

It would require persuasion, smooth talk to the max, but Fowler was convinced he had a shot at luring Reynoso into the United States. A suitcase with one million confiscated dollars was the bait, with promises of more to follow if Reynoso satisfied "John Decker's" nonexistent sponsors and accompanied one major shipment to the drop-off point. A built-in paranoia would prevent the mark from biting instantly, but with a bit of salesmanship—assisted by Dominguez, if he took the bait—it could be done.

Fowler emerged from the air-conditioned house, and the morning heat struck him like a slap across the face. He nearly turned around but a desire to scout the grounds persuaded him to stick it out. Strolling around the courtyard first, he ignored the gardeners at work, his full attention focused on escape routes and the high, surrounding wall. In twenty minutes he had finished off a lazy circuit of the house and come full circle to the covered swimming pool.

Swamp coolers worked here in place of more expensive air-conditioning, but it was better than the heat outside. At first, Jack thought he was alone, but then his eyes picked out a slender figure on the diving board, stock-still and watching Fowler from the far end of the pool.

The woman from the balcony.

Reynoso's woman.

She was dressed—almost—in what appeared to be a crimson string bikini, bright against her olive skin. She gave him a heartbeat to assimilate the vision, then made a graceful dive. Her figure flickered along the bottom of the pool with driving strokes. She surfaced in the shallow end and shook her hair back, elbows resting on the rim of decorative tile.

She regarded Fowler with a cautious smile and asked him, "Do you swim?"

"FROM TIME TO TIME," the gringo answered, moving closer like a man afraid of being bitten by a rattlesnake. "I didn't bring a suit."

"We keep some extras in the locker over there," Maria told him, putting on a practiced smile. "In case you want to change."

"No, thanks." He edged a little closer, staring down at her. "I just had breakfast."

"That's an old wives' tale, you know. About the cramps from eating."

"Oh?"

She pushed off, sidestroked to the ladder, feeling hungry eyes upon her body as she climbed out of the pool. He tried to cover his reaction with a poker face as she ignored her folded towels and came around to shake his hand.

"I am Maria Escobar."

"John Decker," he replied, his eyes dipping to her breasts unconsciously. A tinge of color showed in his cheeks, which might have been arousal or discomfort.

"I saw you yesterday," she said. "You're waiting for Miguel."

It had not been a question, but he felt compelled to answer her. "That's right."

"On business."

"Right again."

"Where do you live in the United States?"

"Miami."

"Ah. The Dolphins."

"You're a football fan?"

Maria shrugged, amused to catch him glancing at her breasts again. "Miguel enjoys the game."

"You don't have many neighbors out here in the sticks."

She caught his meaning, though the turn of phrase was strange to her. "It can be lonely," she agreed. The germ of an idea, implanted in his mind.

"I guess you travel with Miguel."

Maria frowned. "A woman's place is in the home, he says. Do you agree?"

"Depends upon the woman...and the home."

"Sometimes I think it would be nice to get away and visit the United States. Chicago or Los Angeles... perhaps Miami."

"So what's stopping you?"

She shrugged again, and felt the cool air of the pool house tightening her nipples underneath the fabric of her small bikini top. "Miguel would not approve."

"You need permission?"

"It is different in America," she said, not pushing it, but letting her dissatisfaction register a little at a time. "In Mexico, relationships are more...traditional."

"And that's the way you like it." There was skepticism in his tone, enough to give her cautious hope.

"It's how things are, *señor*. You don't mind if I call you John?"

"I'll be insulted if you don't."

"We can't have that."

She led him to a pair of waiting deck chairs and sat with shapely legs stretched out in front of her. Maria followed his fleeting glance and noticed several strands of pubic hair protruding from beneath the taut material of her bikini bottom. Smiling, she shifted slightly to provide him with a better view.

"I'd have to think about it twice, if I were you," he said. "Give up all this to see Chicago or L.A., the novelty wears off and all you've got are dirty streets, some neon after dark."

"The novelty wears off everything," she told him.

"Yeah, I guess that's right."

"Are you opposed to changes, John?"

"Not necessarily. Depends on what I'm changing, and the reasons why."

"You value independence, I can tell."

He frowned. "We all make compromises, every day. The only independent people I've seen lately sleep out on the street."

"At least they aren't in cages."

"No."

His hesitation told Maria she had said too much. Retreating from the razor's edge, she said, "I'm sorry, John. I didn't mean to bore you."

"Not at all. It gives me food for thought."

"Such as?"

He glanced up from her cleavage, smiling. "At the moment, I was thinking that a man can get so wrapped up in his business he forgets about the other end of things at home. He needs to strike a balance."

Gambling, she asked him, "Do you keep a woman in Miami?"

If he was embarrassed by the question, he did not let it show. "Not really. I've been on my own awhile. What makes you ask?"

"You have a certain sensitivity. I think that you could make a woman happy."

"I don't know. I never had much luck before."

"Perhaps a different woman . . ."

"Hey, you never know. I'll keep an open mind."

A distant sound intruded on their conversation, barely audible at first, now growing closer by the moment. It was a helicopter, rotors whipping at the desert air as it approached the landing pad.

"Miguel," she told him simply, rising from her deck chair with a fluid grace that held his eye in spite of the distraction.

He rose and stood beside her, touching-close. "Too bad."

"Perhaps we'll have a chance to talk again before you leave."

"Suits me."

"It's been a pleasure, John."

"The pleasure's mine."

"I mean—"

She touched him, her soft hand on his arm before she seemed to reconsider, shook her head and turned away. It took her three strides to reach the water, and she pushed off into a shallow dive. Momentum took her to the bottom of the pool where she stayed submerged for several moments as she swam its length again with easy, measured strokes.

When she surfaced, he was gone.

MIGUEL IGNACIO REYNOSO always felt his best on coming home. It was not simply the security of his *estancia* that put his mind at ease, but rather knowledge that the land belonged to him. It was *his* land in all directions, spreading out as far as he could see—an empire in the desert, built on blood and sand. It made no difference that his tenants were primarily coyotes, scorpions and gila monsters.

After years of fighting for a foothold in the world, Reynoso had a place to call his own.

The flight to Santa Margarita, off the coast of Baja California, had been worth his time. A syndicate of local smugglers had been running weed to San Diego for the past eight months or so, establishing connections with the local Customs office and enjoying fair success. They had not dabbled in cocaine as yet, but when Reynoso made his first approach, they saw the possibilities.

His reputation had preceded him, ensuring a respectful audience. The *Californios* were eager to expand their operation—and their profits—through association with a major syndicate, and they were wise enough to understand that skimming from Reynoso's end would call the wrath of God down on their heads. A bargain was agreed on, which would benefit them all, Reynoso raking off the lion's share to cover his expenses and expansion of his network from Chihuahua and Sonora to the west. In time the locals might decide they were entitled to a larger slice of pie, but they would be expendable by then, and he could cut them off without damaging his own machine.

Reynoso's pilot circled once around the compound, prior to settling squarely on the helipad. Dominguez was waiting for him in the sunshine, as the rotors started winding down.

"*¿Miguel, qué pasa?*"

"*Muy bien,* Jesús, *¿Usted?*"

"*Bien.*"

A shifting movement near the pool house drew Reynoso's eye in time to see a gringo stranger watching them, one hand raised to shade his eyes.

"*¿Quién es?*"

"A dealer from Miami," said Dominguez. "He was picked up by del Cabo's *federales,* asking questions on the street in Ciudad Juarez."

"You brought him here?"

"His background checks. John Decker, recently paroled for trafficking cocaine in the United States."

"A stranger, all the same."

"He wants to make a deal."

"There are procedures." He was getting angry now.

"He has a million dollars in a bag, Miguel."

Reynoso hesitated, glancing back. The gringo was still in place, with both hands tucked inside his pockets now.

"Maria?"

"In her room, I think."

"The others?"

"Still on schedule. Mapache should be here within the hour, Calderone a little after noon."

"And Trask?"

"No change. He would have telephoned, I'm sure."

"The preparations have been made?"

"As you instructed. Everything is ready for your guests."

"I want some time to freshen up before I meet this dealer from Miami. Bring him to my office in an hour."

"*Sí*, Miguel."

"I hope, for your sake, he is all he seems to be...and nothing more."

"Del Cabo checked him out, Miguel. Our sources in the States—"

Reynoso waved his words away. "We'll find out soon enough," he said. "The last mistake was costly. I will not permit another to impede our progress."

"No, Miguel."

"One hour."

"*Sí*."

He left Dominguez standing in the sun, unwilling to pursue him as Reynoso stepped inside the house. The air-conditioning was heaven, even though it dried a tacky layer of perspiration on his skin.

A shower first, before he went to see Maria. He demanded that she look and smell her best for him, and he would do no less. They had been separated for the past three days, and now Reynoso felt a need he could not ignore. He wondered if Maria ever needed him—or anyone—in quite that way.

No matter.

She was here to serve, and she was well-kept in return. She had begun to learn her place again, but she bore watching, like a stubborn child. If she was not so beautiful...

Reynoso took his time, will overpowering the urgency he felt inside. A man who could not subjugate his passions was a weakling, vulnerable to his enemies, unlike Miguel Reynoso, who had forged his desert empire with a rod of iron and nerves of steel.

He would enjoy Maria soon enough, and in the meantime she could wait while he considered what to do about a gringo from Miami, with a million tax-free dollars in his bag.

9

Fowler was relaxing in his room and thinking of Maria, when Dominguez came to fetch him for a parlay with the man.

"Señor Reynoso asks if you would care to join him in his study," he said, letting Fowler know by his tone that it was not a question he was free to answer in the negative.

"I'd be delighted."

"This way, please."

"Good trip?"

"*¿Señor?*"

"Your boss. I hope he found what he was looking for."

"*El Jefe* has the golden touch."

"That's good to know. I like to back a winner, going in."

"I wish you luck."

"No sweat, I make my own. You have some time to think about that little chat we had last night?"

Dominguez frowned. "Indeed. But as I told you—"

"Sure, I know. Reynoso doesn't ask for your opinion on a deal. Could be that's his mistake."

"*Señor*—"

"I thought we made it 'John.'"

"My first responsibility—"

"Is to the man, I know. And I admire your loyalty," Fowler said. "That doesn't mean you can't look out for number one along the way."

Reynoso's office door was hand-carved oak. Dominguez knocked, and Fowler waited for a muffled voice to beckon them inside.

The room was spacious and luxuriously furnished, which appeared to be the rule for everything Reynoso did. The desk was teak and looked like it would weigh a ton at least. Around the walls, framed landscapes alternated with the mounted heads of wildlife from the desert and surrounding mountains. Mule deer. Bighorn sheep. A ferocious-looking boar flashing six-inch tusks. A jaguar crouched beside the giant desk, about to spring, and Fowler had to do a double take before he realized its eyes were glass, the graceful body stuffed.

Reynoso stood behind the desk with one hand in his pocket, in what seemed to be a deliberate pose. At a glance, he seemed an unimposing man—soft features, with the hairline starting to recede—but there was something in his eyes that put a stop to any snap decisions. Steel beneath the velvet, like a trap concealed.

Dominguez made the introductions, with Reynoso circling around his desk, the bare hint of a smile as he shook Fowler's hand. The dealer's attitude was civil, but he was not giving anything away. When he dismissed Dominguez, Fowler knew he would have to score some points immediately if he planned on staying in the game.

"The first thing I should do," he said, before Reynoso had a chance to speak, "is offer my apologies for moving in on you this way. I planned on waiting up in Ciudad Juarez until you called me, but your man insisted I stay here. If it's inconvenient, with your other deals and all, I'll split right now and we can talk another time."

"There's no time like the present, Señor Decker."

"If you're sure."

"Be seated, please. A drink?"

"Bit early, thanks."

Reynoso nodded, stepped behind his desk again and sank into a high-backed leather chair. "Jesús described the contents of your special luggage and your wish to make a deal. I would prefer to hear the details from the source."

"Well, like I told Señor Dominguez, I've recruited several sponsors who are interested in breaking the Colombian monopoly in southern Florida. If I can find a source that undercuts their wholesale price by three, four thousand on a kilo, I pass the savings on and grab a major portion of their present clientele, along with any new friends I pick up along the way. Of course, I don't expect to earn this privilege without some kickbacks, up the line."

"You have done business with Colombians before, I understand."

"That's right. I stood up on a federal charge, possession with intent, and took the fall alone. The network sent me an attorney who was wet behind the ears. He didn't know his ass from his affidavits, and the prosecution ate him up. Okay, things happen. When I hit the street and asked about my job, the Indians just grin and tell me they don't need me any more. *That* pissed me off."

"And now you want revenge?"

"I want to make a decent living. If a couple of my enemies get scalded in the process, that's a bonus I can handle."

"And if *you* get scalded, Señor Decker?"

"Make it John, okay? I know the risk involved, and I'm prepared to face it. I've got people I can count on when the shit comes down. We ought to do okay... but that's not what you asked me, is it?" Smiling thinly, he continued. "My proposal is, we pay up front for any product you supply *and* kick back two percent of profits for the first twelve months. Your merchandise is paid for, going in, and you lose nothing if the operation blows up in my face. The only way I'd stiff you on the two percent is if I'm dead, in which case you won't have to send your people out to do the job."

"If the Colombians come after me?"

"I can't believe they'd be that loco."

"For a wholesale discount such as you propose, I would expect the rebate to be four percent."

Jack's shoulders slumped. "I'm authorized to offer three. Beyond that point, I have to fly back home and hash it over with my sponsors. They're a little paranoid about the phone, you understand."

Reynoso thought about it for a moment, frowning. "Three percent of gross receipts?"

"What else? I'd have to be an idiot to con you on the net."

"The million dollars?"

"Stays with you," said Fowler. "Call it a down payment or a gesture of respect, whichever you prefer."

"For the amounts of product you will need..."

"We'll have the cash, don't worry. Once we get that powder cut and circulating on the street, the only money problem I expect to have is where to spend it all."

Reynoso stood and came around the desk to shake his hand again. "We have a deal," he said. "The details of delivery and future payments, we can talk about before you leave. Tonight, I have some other guests arriving for a dinner party. It would please me if you joined us...shall we say at nine o'clock?"

"My pleasure, if you're sure I won't be cramping anybody's style."

Reynoso fairly beamed as he replied, "I would not have it any other way."

INSIDE HER LAVISH SUITE, Maria Escobar paced restlessly, like an exotic animal confined against its will. She knew about the evening's banquet, where Reynoso would display her like a household ornament, but she had other pressing matters on her mind.

The gringo, Decker, was an unknown quantity so far. He wanted her, of course—as all men did, on sight—but she could not rely on passion to secure his help in an escape attempt. She had already done the most she could, on short acquaintance, to describe the hell on earth of life beneath Reynoso's thumb. The gringo made a sympathetic noise, but men said anything when they were on a woman's scent. Explicit promises of help were easily forgotten once the itch was scratched, their hunger satisfied. This Decker seemed a different breed so far, but she had learned to trust in no one other than herself.

Assuming he agreed to help her, how would they escape? The gates were guarded, and the walls were hopeless. For a hundred miles or more in each direction, the Chihuahua desert was a perfect killing ground for anyone attempting to elude Reynoso's men. The final straw was that John Decker had arrived in the Mercedes with Dominguez. He was stuck here, at the pleasure of his host, no transportation of his own.

And yet . . .

Depressed but far from giving up, Maria set about the task of getting ready for Miguel's important business dinner. She was nothing but a decoration in the house, predictably dismissed whenever men began discussing things she "would not understand," but there were still ways she could turn the game around.

Miguel, with all his many contradictions, loved displaying her like one of his god-awful mounted trophies, but he seethed with jealous anger if another man responded to the lure. The gringo from Miami would not risk his business and his life to help a peasant woman he had never met before that afternoon.

Unless Maria made it worth his time.

And that, she thought, could be arranged in many ways.

She was surprised to feel an honest smile, perhaps the first one in a month, turn up the corners of her mouth. She did not have a full plan yet, but she was getting there. From this point on, the outcome depended on the other guests, their temperament, and any secrets locked up in Reynoso's mind.

She did not hear him enter, silent at a cat, and she was startled when she turned in the direction of her bedroom and found him standing there. During the four years of her captivity, this was just the second time Reynoso had set foot inside her private room. It had to be excitement or the worst of news, and she could almost flip a coin to see which she preferred.

"Take off your clothes," he said. "I need you. Now."

She faced him for a moment, feeling ice begin to crystalize inside her body, numbing her. When she was properly anesthetized, Maria forced a smile and did as she was told.

EMILIO MAPACHE HATED flying—most especially in helicopters—but the endless desert-mountain-desert drive from Hermosillo took too long, a kind of ordeal in itself. This way, if something happened to them in the air, at least he would not have to walk for fifty miles in search of gasoline.

The helicopter and its pilot were Reynoso's property, a gesture of convenience with a warning tucked inside. If anything went wrong this weekend, there was no way out.

Things *had* been bad for business lately in Sonora. Customs agents and the DEA were cracking down along the Arizona border, putting undercover agents on the streets of Cananea and Nogales. There had been arrests and seizures in unusual numbers, but the border stretched for long, unguarded miles beyond the scattering of towns, and dope was getting through.

As always.

Reynoso would be angry at the recent losses, further outraged by the fact that DEA had placed a man inside his own back yard at Ciudad Juarez. The bastard had been weeded out, but it was still a point of honor with Miguel, reflecting on his general competence. If the narcotics agent had secured promotion in the family beyond the status of a lowly runner, then Miguel's subordinates would have been forced to ask some pointed questions their *patrón* could not ignore.

But he had saved the day—or cut their losses, anyhow—and now it would be someone else in trouble, waiting for the ax to fall. Reynoso did not party as a rule, and in the years Mapache had been working for him, he had never thrown a banquet at his home without some hidden motive, such as punishment of insubordinate lieutenants, a demand for the immediate return of misappropriated funds.

Four banquets in as many years, and each time there was sudden justice for dessert. Invited guests would know the menu, going in, but none of them would dare refuse, a gesture certain to confirm their guilt—assuming that Miguel suspected them of anything.

Mapache clenched his teeth as he beheld the desert fortress of Miguel Reynoso several miles ahead. The troops would have them pegged on radar, just in case they turned out hostile and the *federales* had not beamed a warning out ahead of time. They drew no gunfire as they crossed the heavy wall, but sentries had them neatly bracketed with automatic rifles, shotguns, submachine guns, when they touched down on the helipad.

A troop of airborne raiders would have been shot down at once... or riddled in their tracks once they were on the ground. Fine sport, if you could stand the heat.

No stranger to the heat himself, Mapache shook hands with Jesús Dominguez when his feet were back in touch with Mother Earth.

"Miguel?"

"Inside," Reynoso's first lieutenant said. "He's waiting for you."

"And the others?"

"On their way."

They reached the house and stepped inside. Mapache hoped it was the air-conditioning that made a sudden chill race down his spine.

LUPE CALDERONE WAS SICK and tired of driving by the time they reached Chihuahua, rolling north across the barren desert flats. His BMW limousine was air-conditioned, but the heat outside was something else, almost a sentient thing, with lethal tricks in store for any fool who stopped out here, long miles from anywhere.

It was the long way out of Texas, leaving Houston on the day before and stopping for a change of wheels at San Antonio. They crossed the border at Del Rio, rolling west across Coahuila toward Chihuahua and their final stop before the last leg of their journey. Calderone knew they were still on time, but meeting with Reynoso always made him nervous, fearful that he might say something wrong—offend the man somehow—and wind up feeding maggots in a shallow grave.

Try as he might, it was impossible to know what trigger incident would set Reynoso off. They had experienced a minor fluctuation in the profit margin lately, spanning western Texas and a portion of New Mexico, with local sheriffs cracking down across the board, but Calderone was turning it around by slow degrees. *Too* slow, perhaps, to satisfy Reynoso, but the frontier days of killing marshals in the street and taking over desert towns were history. He missed the good old days sometimes, but there was nothing he could do to bring them back.

Reynoso was a man of common sense, and he was bound to understand. Calderone shrugged as he reassured himself that the man could not blame his representatives at large because some stupid high school bitch OD'd and parents started screaming for their overpaid elected politicians to declare a local "war on drugs." In time the grief and anger would inevitably fade, and he could use the interim to strengthen ties with various departments where the cops were sadly overworked and underpaid. A simple deal with Calderone meant money in the pocket, plus relief from filling out the reams of paperwork demanded every time the deputies uncovered a substantial cache of drugs.

And, it was not as though they were really *winning* anything, diverting this or that consignment of cocaine. The cops knew—everybody knew—that close to ninety-four percent of contraband dispatched to the United States was getting through. Why should a local yokel bust his hump for fifteen minutes in the weekly paper and a commendation letter in his file, when he could save himself the effort, simply look the other way, and make some decent spending money on the side.

Greed made the world go round, and it was spinning faster all the time.

Reynoso had to understand that the problems they were having with police along the border were a fact of life, a built-in risk that came with doing business on the wrong side of the law. He had placed Calderone in charge of Texas and New Mexico, to manage his affairs, but no one had believed the enterprise would come down trouble-free. At home in Mexico, Reynoso had been having problems of his own, with infiltrators from the DEA, but no one blamed Miguel for letting a narcotics agent slip inside his guard.

The trouble with progressive logic was that sometimes, in a fit of rage, Miguel forgot about the niceties of common sense and let emotion take control. He never screamed or ranted at his enemies, but he was deadly in a clinch. At such times, there was nothing anyone could do but stay out of his way and let the fury run its course, then pick up the dead when he returned to something like normality.

Not me, thought Calderone. It can't be me he wants this time.

Or could it?

For the hundredth time since leaving, he was torn between the need to forge ahead and a desire to have his driver turn the car around, make tracks for any compass point that led him safely from Chihuahua and the reach of an employer he had come to fear.

The last bit, feeling frightened, was enough to guarantee that Calderone would not turn back. If nothing else, he had to prove his manhood on a private level, facing down Reynoso in his own back yard, if it came down to that.

And if it didn't . . . then, he was prepared to celebrate and wear a happy face, regardless of the other guests selected on the basis of their negligence or treason to become examples for the family. The best part of a public lynching was relaxing in the certain knowledge that you would not be among the victims stretching rope.

Not this time.

He had served Reynoso well, in Texas and New Mexico. If any man said otherwise, it would be his responsibility to prove the charge and make it stick.

Prepared for anything, the dealer felt a new wave of anxiety, intent on getting to his destination, putting sand and asphalt well behind him for a time. He tapped the driver's shoulder, asked if they could manage better speed and felt the BMW surge ahead.

Another hour, give or take, and he would see Reynoso face-to-face, shake hands and read the message in those viper's eyes. If it was life, so much the better for everyone. If it was death . . . well, Lupe Calderone still had a few surprises up his sleeve. A trick or two Reynoso may have overlooked or else forgotten on his swift climb to the top.

Old tricks were every bit as good as new ones, when they worked.

And this one was a killer, all the way.

10

The banquet was a semiformal gathering, which spared Jack Fowler the necessity of standing up for alterations on a borrowed tuxedo. He wore a stylish, lightweight suit, French cuffs with diamond links that had been confiscated from a jewelry-conscious dealer in Fort Lauderdale six months before. His tie was silk, his shoes were Gucci, and the CIA commando dagger didn't even make a wrinkle in his pocket when he tucked it out of sight.

As Fowler dressed, he thought about the new arrivals he had glimpsed that afternoon. Both Hispanic, but of very different types. The first was five foot nothing, stocky, with a brooding face, big hands, his black hair sprayed into a stiff pompadour. A helicopter dropped him off a little after noon, with Dominguez waiting on the pad to shake his hand and usher him inside. From the expression on the short man's face, he either hated flying or the visit to Reynoso's spread was not a pleasure trip.

The second pilgrim made it Mutt and Jeff. Arriving in a chauffeured luxury sedan two hours later, he unfolded to an easy six foot three and probably weighed 180 pounds with three-piece suit and shoes included. If the first guest was a bludgeon, this one had to be a straight-edged razor, lean and lethal—from the creases in his clothing to his perfect smile. He wore his hair cut short enough to comb with a ton of grease and cultivated a neatly trimmed mustache. Dominguez was on hand once more as the official greeter, while a rifleman directed the chauffeur around in back.

Jack knew his way down to the dining room by now, and he did not wait for Reynoso's houseman to escort him. Stepping into the adjacent lounge, he found Reynoso and Dominguez sipping beer from tall, thin glasses. Caught between them, clinging to a glass of wine, Maria Escobar was lovely in a low-cut velvet dress with diamonds at the throat.

"Ah, Señor Decker... you must meet my fiancée. Maria Escobar, John Decker, from Miami, Florida."

"*Con mucho gusto,* Señor Decker."

"The pleasure is mine, *señorita.*"

If Dominguez and Reynoso didn't know about the morning's poolside meeting, Fowler had no plans to fill them in. He was not certain of Maria's game, but something flickered in her dark eyes when Reynoso introduced her as his fiancée. Jack did not know the lady well enough to say if it had been amusement or contempt.

The other guests showed up a moment later, just as Fowler poured himself a beer. Emilio Mapache was the fireplug with the pompadour. His handshake was something in the nature of a challenge to the gringo, showing Fowler there was muscle buried underneath the outer layer of flab. The gentleman was Lupe Calderone, a name that Fowler vaguely recognized from background briefings on the drug trade out of Texas and New Mexico, through southern California. Calderone did not shake hands but made a courtly little bow.

The butler showed them in to dinner, with Reynoso seated at the table's head, Dominguez at his right hand and Maria on his left. Jack sat beside Maria at their host's direction, separating her from Calderone. Mapache took a seat directly opposite, ignoring Fowler as he ordered a tequila.

When all of them had drinks at hand, Reynoso stood and raised his glass. "I'm happy each of you could join me here tonight," he said. "Emilio, from his work in Hermosillo. Lupe, all the way from Houston, where his business has begun to prosper. The surprise addition of our new amigo from Miami, Señor Decker. I believe we shall do great things together in the months ahead."

"I'm counting on it," Fowler told him with a smile.

"And to the only woman in my life, whose beauty is such that I still find it difficult to realize that she has chosen me, above all other men."

Maria's smile seemed forced, and Fowler noticed that she barely sipped her wine in answer to Reynoso's toast. He thought about the comments she had made beside the pool, putting in mind the image of a sleek bird in a gilded cage, and pushed the problem out of mind to concentrate on his objective of the moment.

Anything he could learn about Reynoso's visitors might come in handy later on. A point of leverage for investigators in their separate cities, something to connect them with established crimes.

And in the process, he would shop around for hints on how to play Reynoso, hook him for a meet on U.S. soil— or close enough to grab, at any rate—the first time he delivered Fowler's merchandise.

Right now, he welcomed any handle he could find.

It just might be enough to get him through the night alive.

THERE WAS a minimum of conversation as they worked their way through appetizers, soup and salad, toward the steak and lobster tails Reynoso's chef had lovingly prepared for the main course. Maria kept her answers brief and cordial when she was addressed directly, otherwise content to let the men hold forth.

She knew them all. Mapache was a thug from Mazatlán, in Sinaloa, where he grew up on the streets and overcame his size by sheer ferocity. His reputation as a brutal fighter ultimately made displays unnecessary, and the ever-present threat of violence served him well in his vocation as a marijuana smuggler, dealing with the gringos who came south to score a load of dreams. Mapache had a dozen murders to his credit by the time he graduated to cocaine, and the Reynoso syndicate decided he was worth more on the payroll than in prison... or the grave. Supported by Reynoso's guns and cash, Mapache moved to Hermosillo, in Sonora, where he swiftly crushed the competition and established new routes into the United States. These days he dealt with buyers in Nogales, Tucson, Phoenix, San Diego and Los Angeles, maintaining order on the western fringes of Reynoso's empire with an execution now and then to keep himself in shape.

In contrast to Mapache, Calderone was something of a dandy, more concerned about his dress and grooming, keeping up with all the latest styles. Maria knew that his appearance was deceptive, though; a glossy mask that hid the rot inside. A native of Durango, Calderone had knifed his sister's pimp to death when he was twelve years old, and there had been at least two dozen other slayings in the intervening years. He favored knives, but in emergencies the end was more important than the means. Recruited by Miguel as an enforcer, Calderone had quickly demonstrated a surprising business sense that moved him up the ladder from a lowly soldier to a prime lieutenant in the family. His ultimate reward had been the recent relocation to *El Norte,* where he managed cocaine sales in Texas and New Mexico.

Maria did not know John Decker yet, but she had seen his type before. The gringos who approached Miguel were mostly dealers who had carved a territory for themselves in the United States and came looking for a steady source to keep themselves on top. Miami meant Colombians, the kind of competition that could lead to war, and while she would not mourn Reynoso's death, she could not wait around in hope that someone would get lucky this time, when assassins had so often failed before.

She could grow old and gray while waiting for Miguel to stumble, drop his guard, and she had wasted time enough already as it was. Attempting to escape might cost her life next time, but she no longer cared.

Each day spent with Miguel Reynoso was a living death.

The steak was tender, rare; the lobster succulent. Maria hardly tasted any of it, concentrating on her plans for Decker and the need to speak with him alone once more. It would be doubly difficult, with other guests on hand, but logic told her she was running out of time. His business might consume another day or two at most, and then he would be gone. A slender hope evaporating when he left.

She knew Miguel would send for her tonight, as always when he entertained associates. It strengthened him somehow—to prove himself a man, as he was forced to deal with other men—and she would have no opportunity to visit Decker's room before the dawn. Perhaps, she mused, if they had any free time in the afternoon...

She finished, leaving more than she had eaten, waiting for the others. Calderone and Decker cleaned their plates, and Mapache was working on a second steak while his companions sipped their drinks, pretending not to notice. The dessert was *flan,* a creamy custard bathed in caramel, which she accepted out of habit, barely tasting it before she laid her spoon aside.

Reynoso liked her slim, but she had reasons of her own for keeping fit. Less weight to slow her down when she was running for her life.

"Maria?"

She restrained herself from jumping when Reynoso took her hand in his. Her smile was automatic, the result of practice and conditioning.

"You all have business to discuss," she said, reciting from the script she knew by heart. "If you'll excuse me, I'll retire and leave you to it."

Rising from her chair, Maria took a chance to brush her hip against John Decker's sleeve as she retreated, something to distract him as he listened to Miguel.

Tomorrow, if things worked out, she would have time and opportunity to speak with him alone. A risk that she would gladly take.

Perhaps it would be the last chance she would ever have to save herself.

THE BUTLER CLEARED their plates away, brought coffee, then disappeared. Reynoso would not be disturbed again unless he rang the bell for service. He had swept the room for bugs, as was his practice before a business conference, and found it clean. The words he spoke from this point on would go no farther than the men who shared his table and who were waiting for him to begin.

"A man with friends is never poor," he said, regarding each of them in turn. "New friends or old, the one thing without which a man survives, but never truly lives.

Our friendships make us strong, if we choose well. They keep us warm on bitter nights and shelter us on stormy days. In business and in private life, the bonds of friendship guarantee fidelity and trust, unshakable, beyond misfortune and adversity."

The others watched him, seemingly at ease, but their innards were in the tight grip of anxiety. Dominguez knew where he was going; Decker clearly did not have a clue. As for the others...

"Friendship is a two-edged sword, however," he continued, rising from his chair. Eyes followed him as he began to pace around the dining room. "If we are careless in selecting those we trust, betrayal is the ultimate reward. A man whose friends desert him in a time of trial is left with nothing, stripped of dignity and hope."

Reynoso paused beside a full suit of Castilian armor that stood in one corner of the room, his finger sliding gingerly around the pommel of the heavy sword. He seemed distracted from his topic, but his mind was focused with a clarity few men attained, before the moment of their death.

"Aside from Señor Decker, who is new to our fraternity, we have been friends for years," he said. "I trust each one of you as I would trust my own blood, a brother or a son. The life I have depends on each of you in turn, as your lives finally depend on me."

He gave the sword a tug and pulled it free. No visible reaction was displayed by his guests as he continued on his way, making a lazy circuit of the table, pausing now and then to swing the sword at empty air.

"Such trust is paramount in the affairs of men," he said. "The bold conquistadors who won our homeland from the godless savages relied on one another every day. Their steadfast courage offered a united front against their countless enemies, and they prevailed. It was not steel or gunpowder that made our country great." Reynoso paused and tapped his chest above the heart. "It was the soul of honor in our ancestors that makes us men."

Approaching Decker on the flank, he watched the gringo closely, looking for a hint of nervousness and found none. Next to the dealer from Miami, Lupe Calderone was listening intently, an inquisitive expression on his face.

Reynoso nodded with grave satisfaction, then paused behind his own chair, leaning on the sword as if it were a walking stick. Its sharp point rested on the hardwood floor between his feet.

"It grieves me to announce that we have been betrayed," he said at last. The silence was taut in the room as he hesitated, eyeing each in turn. "One of our own has turned against us in pursuit of private gain, a pig who sells his brothers for a pocketful of silver and the hope of ruling all, one day."

He was on the prowl again, with slow steps covering the floor, the sword a weightless nothing in his hands.

"One man decides to help himself at the expense of those who trust him, and we suffer equally. Betrayal shames each one of us until the traitor is unmasked and duly punished for his crime."

No answer came from the Judas—whoever he was—or the innocents who shared his space.

"If there was a defense for treason, any explanation for betrayal of a friend and brother, I would gladly listen and forgive. The money stolen is as nothing in comparison to the disgrace we share, with our own selling out his family."

Another moment was spent waiting, knowing in his heart the gutless bastard would not speak out in his own defense. He must be gambling, even now, on a mistake or pure dumb luck to shield him from the retribution he deserved.

"So be it."

Though the words were barely whispered, they were audible to every member of the dinner party as Reynoso raised the sword, both arms above his head, and spun around to face Emilio Mapache. Finally, too late, the fat man raised an arm to shield his face, but the sharp blade sliced through his radius and ulna to lodge in his skull above one ear.

Mapache twitched and shuddered, crimson spouting from the mortal wound. The fingers of his severed hand clenched tight, a dying spider's legs, and then relaxed. Jesús Dominguez flinched away, blood spattering his shirt and jacket, as Reynoso tugged the long sword free and struck again.

And yet again.

The third stroke finished it. Mapache was staring at himself, his head inverted in the bloody swamp of his lap, the piggy eyes gone out of focus and glazing over as the final sentient spark winked out.

Reynoso stepped back, found his handiwork sufficient, and turned to the others.

"Two weeks ago," Reynoso told his now-smaller audience, "a shipment to Nogales disappeared without a trace. Mapache claimed it had been stolen by a band of renegades. In fact, he took it for himself and sold the product in Los Angeles, believing I would never learn the truth. You see the end result of his mistake."

Dominguez finished daubing bloodstains from his face and put the handkerchief away. No comment came from the three survivors as Reynoso stood before them, leaning on his sword.

"Our business is concluded for this evening," he declared. "If you would be so kind as to excuse us, Señor Decker, we will speak at greater length tomorrow afternoon."

"I'd rather help," Fowler said. "That is, if you don't mind. I see you've got some cleaning up to do."

Reynoso smiled.

"As you prefer, my friend."

THEY WRAPPED Mapache's body and its severed pieces in a plastic tarp. The dead weight was something to contend with, even split up four ways. Reynoso and Dominguez took the lead, with Calderone and Fowler bringing up the rear, four porters taking out the garbage in the dead of night.

A brilliant desert moon provided ample light, and Dominguez fetched shovels from a toolshed after they had stashed Mapache in the trunk of Calderone's sedan. Communal effort, all the way.

Initial shock aside, Jack Fowler had recovered quickly, drawing on his long acquaintanceship with violent death to see him past the moment. Offering to help them dump the corpse had been a brainstorm, the reaction of his host the only necessary confirmation of a choice well made. Complicity was something each of them would understand.

They drove for twenty minutes, using headlights past the gates, with swooping bats and startled rabbits flitting through the double beams. Their destination was a dry arroyo two miles out from the *estancia,* and Fowler had the feeling that Dominguez, behind the wheel, could have found it with his eyes closed.

Some of them had passed this way before.

The grave was deep enough to cover up Mapache's bulk, but the loose earth would prove insufficient to deter attack by scavengers. If anything, Reynoso would be counting on the desert dwellers for their contribution in disposing of his kill. The grave itself and the tumbleweeds Dominguez scattered carelessly around it were a mere concession to propriety, a civilized facade.

He did not need to ask about the disposition of Mapache's territory, knowing that Reynoso would have lined up a successor in advance, before he issued invitations to the hood's last supper. Somewhere, probably in Hermosillo or Nogales, someone else was celebrating his promotion while they dumped Mapache's pitiful remains.

And life went on for some.

He had the makings of a murder charge against Reynoso now, but it would have to stick in local court, and that meant waiting for the *federales* to bestir themselves. A waste of time, in Fowler's view, when he could take Reynoso down for twenty-five to life for trafficking in the United States.

But first he had to get the bastard there.

A slow drive back and Fowler knew enough to keep his mouth shut, leaving his companions with the pale illusion of a funeral party, occupied with private thoughts.

Tomorrow.

It was soon enough to hash the details over with Reynoso, trying to convince him of the need for just one fleeting visit to the States. Rehearsal time, and he would sell the plan as if his very life depended on the dealer's choice.

And, Fowler thought, it might at that.

11

The trip had not been Clinton Trask's idea of a vacation, but a man did what he had to do. *The Book of Eastwood,* Chapter 4, Verse 17. Amen.

The thought of using his vacation time to visit Mexico—much less Miguel Reynoso—frankly turned his stomach, but the outing had become an absolute necessity. His sick time and accumulated leave were sitting there, just staring Clinton in the face, and when the shit came down, he knew what was required.

It was his own damned fault, of course. The gambling started small, took hold of something in your head when you weren't looking, grew by frantic leaps and bounds before a man knew what the hell was happening. A football game or two to start. The horses now and then. Then every time, no matter where the fucking nags were running. Dog tracks. Basketball and hockey. The Olympic Games. World Series time.

Word gets around.

A man who's up to bet on anything and everything will find no end of opportunities available. An occasional floating game in Houston, or there were always places he could go across the border if he felt a sudden urge to throw his cash away. It was against the law to bet on presidential votes, but what the hell? Dukakis cost him seven grand in 1988, and it was pure poetic justice when the bastard's wife went into detox for the umpteenth time.

Of course, it wasn't easy, keeping up a solid front when the only thing he ever seemed to pick were losers. Alimony payments were a bitch—much like his wife, in fact—and even God himself was not averse to fixing contests, when he knew Trask had some money riding on the line. No one could tell him that the Giants weren't in shape to beat the Oakland A's before a fucking earthquake broke their stride and drove them out of Candlestick.

And, yes, word got around.

The money crunch came out of nowhere, eating up his bank account and Uncle Jacob's trust fund like a swarm of termites in a pile of rotten lumber. One day it was there; the next—or so it seemed—he had been talking terms with Eddie Cole and setting up a loan outside the normal channels, where it wouldn't show on anybody's books. The IRS, for instance.

It should have been enough to sober Trask, the vigorish alone, but he was caught up in the spin by that point. One good score would see him out of debt and in the black. His luck was bound to change in time.

It did. From bad to worse.

Now, Eddie Cole was nice enough to talk to on a social basis, but he was not one to cross on a business deal. If thirteen thousand was due on Monday next, at twenty-five percent per week, the cash would either be available, or Eddie Cole better have something to believe in. He kept a team of pet gorillas on the payroll—grade-school dropouts who had mastered certain basic phrases, such as "Where's the money, motherfucker?"—and he fed them welshers when the stock of T-bone steaks ran low. One visit from the wrecking crew was normally enough to make a blind man see the light, but Trask was seemingly immune from punishment, and he had wondered why.

He only wondered until the afternoon Jesús Dominguez clued him in.

In simple terms, it went like this: Dominguez and his master—one Miguel Reynoso of Chihuahua—had a piece of Eddie Cole, investing in the loan shark business as a variation on their normal trade in contraband. As luck would have it, Cole had mentioned Trask one afternoon when they were talking shop, and the idea was born. Reynoso bought Trask's paper, keeping the gorillas off his back, and sent Jesús around instead to break the news. He could come aboard as a partner, meaning Trask could kiss his debt goodbye and make some money on the side, providing he saw fit to play along and follow orders.

The alternatives were grim. If Trask rejected the arrangement, he had some other options: pay off his debt at once in full; or drop dead—a process that Dominguez estimated might take several days, if his employees were meticulous and very careful with their power tools. Another avenue, going public with the whole damned story, offered Trask the extra twist of personal disgrace and prosecution while he waited for Reynoso's men to track him down and crush him like an insect.

At first he tried to reason with the Mexicans, but he was talking to the wall. Reynoso loved the notion of the DEA assistant supervisor trotting on a leash, and he would not be swayed by arguments or empty promises. The deal was carved in stone.

A man who knew his limitations, Clinton Trask had played along.

At first the information was a minor tidbit, here and there. The timing and location of a scheduled raid, providing the intended targets with sufficient opportunity to move their stash. A briefing on the issuance of warrants or the evidential details tucked away in sealed indictments. "Inside" morsels a defense attorney could produce to shake the credibility of witnesses in state or federal court.

It took a while for Trask to graduate to homicide.

In fact, he must have known that it would be inevitable, fingering the odd informant and directing shooters to the "safe" address where he was stashed away. Reynoso's team enjoyed a sudden run of luck, eliminating pesky witnesses who could have cramped their style if they had lived to testify. When Trask allowed himself to think about it—he was drinking more these days and gambling less—he told himself that he was merely looking out for number one.

With Hector Elizalde, it was different. Trask was in so deep and owed so much by then that it was hopeless, but the pain of giving up a brother agent—as opposed to lowlife dealers singing for immunity to save themselves—had kept him up at nights. The afternoon he looked at photographs of Elizalde's body, Trask had contemplated suicide. The .38 was in his hand before he realized that checking out would not bring Hector back.

Instead Trask took the money he received for selling Hector out—at least, most of it, there was a Lakers game he couldn't miss—and wiped each bill for prints. He wore rubber kitchen gloves the night he tucked it in an envelope, addressed to Elizalde's widow in McAllen, Texas. To cover his ass, he even used a sponge and water from the tap, so the forensics boys would come up empty when they tried to type his blood from dried saliva on the envelope and stamp.

But now something else was in the wind.

Another bit of news, however fragmentary, and an urgent summons from Reynoso. This time, God knows why, the bastard was insisting on a face-to-face.

Trask did his best to keep it casual. A minor family problem out in Phoenix, no big deal. He had vacation time saved up, and there was nothing special going on around the office that a flunky couldn't handle for the next few days. The overnight approval was a rubber stamp from Grady Sears, and Trask was on his way.

The way to handle a lie was to cover every angle, or it blew up in your face. First thing, he booked a hotel room in Phoenix, paying with a credit card for five days in advance. If anybody called, they would discover he was registered, and Trask would check in once a day or so to see if there were any messages demanding a response. As soon as he had registered and left a bag to make the room look lived-in, Trask had turned his rental compact south on Highway 10 to Tucson, and went on from there to cross the border at Nogales, with a tourist card and driver's license in the name of "Joseph Blake." The next two hundred miles took him southeast from there, and he was closing in.

There was no point insisting that he couldn't name the mark this time, or even give a vague description to the troops. Reynoso wanted him on site, having in mind some half-assed plan to weed the infiltrator out. Trask had no choice but to agree. He told himself Reynoso was not fool enough to kill the golden goose, but who could say for sure?

Trask had his mind made up. It was the last time he would play for human lives, and if Reynoso didn't like it, he could damn well pull the plug. There came a point for any man, when nothing anybody else could do would rival self-inflicted pain. Trask understood that he was

swiftly gaining on the point of no return, and it was time
to turn his life around . . . or simply hit the brakes.

Once more, and out.

No matter what it cost.

THE MUFFLED KNOCKING on his door took Fowler by
surprise. He was just heading for the shower, the breakfast dishes having been recently cleared away. He pulled
a robe on over Jockey shorts and tied the belt around his
waist as he approached the door.

"May I come in?"

Maria Escobar slid past him as she spoke, not waiting
for an answer. Fowler checked the empty hall outside and
closed the door behind her, double-locking it.

"Is something wrong?"

She turned and took him in with an appraising glance.
"I'm sorry if I interrupted anything," she said. "It's urgent that I speak to you."

"So, speak."

"May I sit down?"

"You got this far."

She took it as a yes and settled in the only chair. Jack
chose a corner of the unmade bed.

"I need your help," Maria told him.

"Oh?"

"To get away."

He felt the short hairs stirring on his nape. It could
have been a test, some kind of setup, or an honest plea.
Whatever, he had everything to lose and nothing ob-
vious to gain by swallowing the line.

"Away from what?"

"Miguel. This place. I am a prisoner, *señor.*"

"Oh, yes?"

"You must believe me. There is no time to explain, but I am *not* Miguel's fiancée. He is holding me against my will."

"That's something you forgot to mention yesterday."

"I did not know you well enough to take the chance."

"And now you do?"

"I have no choice. Tomorrow or the next day you will leave. It may be months before Miguel has other visitors from the United States. I cannot wait. If you won't help me . . . I must find another way."

She left the threat of desperate action hanging there between them, Fowler studying her eyes and searching hopelessly for indicators of sincerity before he caught himself.

What difference did it make, regardless? Either she was testing him, or she was asking the impossible.

"We've got a couple problems," he informed her. "First, I'm talking business with Miguel, and it's important that I don't do anything to queer the deal. That's one. The other is, Dominguez drove me down from Ciudad Juarez, so even if I bought your story—and you haven't sold me yet—there's nothing I can do. You won't exactly fit inside my luggage, and I think Jesús may notice if you're sitting in the car."

Maria bit her lip, a frown of concentration turning down the corners of her mouth.

"If I persuade Miguel to let me ride along—some shopping let us say, in Ciudad Juarez—would you assist me then?"

"The truth is, I'm a businessman. I didn't travel all the way from Florida to interrupt a lover's quarrel."

"It's money that you care about?"

"I'm not in business for my health."

"But there are other ways to pay a debt, *señor*."

She rose and crossed the room to stand in front of Fowler, fingers rising to the buttons of her blouse. She had the first two open, showing cleavage by the time he spoke.

"Maria—"

"You have no one special in Miami," she reminded him. "I could be yours. There are so many ways I could make you happy, John."

The blouse slid down her arms, no bra beneath it. Cupping perfect breasts, Maria stroked the nipples with her thumbs until they stood erect.

If she was acting, Fowler had to wonder what had happened to Reynoso's fabled jealousy. It was a long way from a simple sales pitch to his woman stripping down in front of strangers, offering herself as a reward for challenging the odds.

Her slacks were snug around the waist, but loose below. They dropped around her ankles once Maria got them past her hips, and Fowler had a glimpse of heaven as she kicked them to the side. The fabric must have been agreeable to tender flesh, for she wore nothing underneath.

Alarms were going off in Fowler's skull, but he did not resist Maria when she took his hand and wedged it in between her legs. The woman seared him with her heat, despite the dampness there. She leaned into Fowler, with her free hand cupped behind his head, and brought a straining nipple to his lips.

She found the belt of his terry robe and tugged it open, groping for him, fingers circling his shaft and setting him on fire. He could not protest with his mouth full, and the plain truth was that he did not feel much like arguing, in any case. Maria pressed him backward on the rumpled bedclothes, going with him, straddling his waist and sliding backward, for position. When she tucked him up inside her, wriggling backward, Fowler caught his breath and closed his eyes in surrender.

At first the new disturbance seemed to come from far away, like faint knocking, and he instantly mistook it for the echo of his heartbeat pounding in his skull. The truth sank in a moment later, when Maria lost her rhythm, faltering, and clapped a sweaty hand across his mouth.

"¿Señor? Perdóneme usted."

He had trouble getting his voice, but he finally got it as Maria scrambled clear.

"Hang on a sec. I'll be right there."

It was Dominguez at the door, and Fowler's mind went into a spin.

If they had sent Maria to entrap him, would the weasel still be knocking, calling him politely, when he could have kicked the door or used a passkey just as easily and caught them in the act? It didn't play, but Fowler had no time to scan the different angles as he snatched his robe together, moving toward the door. Maria was safe inside the bathroom by the time he got there.

"Yes?"

"Señor Reynoso needs to speak with you," Dominguez said. "At once."

"Okay if I get dressed?"

Dominguez smiled without a trace of humor in his eyes. "An excellent idea. But quickly, please."

"Sure thing."

It took about five minutes. Maria was still invisible and strictly on her own as Fowler joined Dominguez in the hall. A shooter was standing to the side and watching both of them, a pistol bulging underneath his sport coat. Fowler had not seen him previously.

"After you."

Dominguez took the lead, his shadow falling in behind to make a sandwich. Fowler had an inkling it could only be bad news, but he refused to speculate upon disaster in advance. Whatever scene he had to play, the act would be a trifle more convincing if he was surprised for real.

No problem there.

Reynoso met him in the study, as before, the jaguar standing guard beside his massive desk. This time, the glass eyes seemed to follow Fowler as he crossed the room and took a seat. The cat seemed prepared to spring and maul him at an order from Reynoso's lips.

"I trust your sleep was undisturbed," Reynoso said, relaxing in his high-backed leather chair.

"I don't have nightmares," Fowler told him.

"So, a pristine conscience."

"Not exactly. Let's just say blood doesn't bother me. I don't believe in ghosts."

"Do you believe in luck?"

"I think we make our own. The good and bad alike."

Reynoso frowned. "An interesting hypothesis. If you're correct, I must be doing something wrong."

"How's that?"

"My luck has turned, apparently. Last week I found a federal agent posing as a member of my family. No sooner is the pig disposed of than I find another, sent to take his place."

"Shit happens," Fowler said, his stomach churning. "That's the way they took me down in Florida, a while back. It wasn't my arrangement, but I went ahead and made delivery regardless. Turned out I was handing product over to the fucking DEA."

"And where was it you served your time again?" Reynoso asked.

"Atlanta."

"Ah."

"Is there a problem here? I mean, Dominguez told me your *federales* checked me out in Ciudad Juarez. I shouldn't even *be* here if my background didn't scan."

"That's true enough."

Reynoso did not seem to move, but Fowler knew he must have touched a hidden button, for a portion of the bookcase at his back swung open, running smooth on well-oil hinges, and a middle-aged American stepped out of what appeared to be a walk-in closet minus clothes.

"Miami. An ex-convict. Cash in hand." Reynoso spoke the words like he was running down a checklist in his mind. "Coincidence, perhaps?"

Jack cocked an eyebrow at the new arrival, noticing a sheen of perspiration on his forehead. "What coincidence?" he asked. "Who's this?"

"Forgive my lapse of etiquette," Reynoso said. "John Decker from Miami, meet my good friend Clinton Trask, from Houston, Texas. Clinton holds the rank of an assistant supervisor in the DEA."

A flash, and Fowler saw it all. His cover blown to pieces as he sat there, playing dumb. The leak in Houston, Stano's bosom buddy telling just the necessary few about their plan. No names, of course, but clues enough to put Reynoso on his guard against a gringo from Miami bearing gifts of cash.

The stutter of a heartbeat, and he knew that he was fucked, with nothing left to lose. Unthinking, blinded by a burst of rage, Jack launched himself at Clinton Trask, his fingers hooked like claws to lock around the slimy bastard's throat and wreak the most destruction he could manage in the seconds that remained.

He almost made it, kissing-close to contact when Reynoso came alive and swung the blackjack he produced from out of nowhere, dead on target as he clipped Jack's skull behind the ear.

A Ferris wheel of light spun once around in Fowler's head, and then went dark. He never felt the impact as he crumpled to the floor, facedown in front of Clinton Trask.

12

The world was upside down when Fowler woke to alternating pain and nausea, alternating waves of misery that overlapped and combined with dizziness to drag him in and out of consciousness. It took a moment for the groggy man to realize that *he* was hanging upside down, suspended somehow by his knees, and then the nausea took over, bringing back his breakfast in a rush. Instinctively he turned his head and held his breath to keep from aspirating vomit until the moment passed.

Jack told himself it was a natural reaction to the knockout blow he had received. The pain was centered in his skull, his wrists, behind his knees, and the combination told Fowler that he was suspended from a so-called "parrot's perch"—a crude trapeze that left him hanging, wrists and ankles cuffed together, with his head down toward the floor.

A concrete floor at that, from all appearances. His eyes came into focus on a metal drain directly under him. The grate was stained with rust . . . or something else.

A slaughterhouse.

His clothes were gone; the air-conditioning raised goose bumps on his naked flesh. A bat's eye view of cinder blocks and open space gave Fowler reason to believe that he was hanging in the basement, since his tour of the compound had revealed no similar construction on the grounds. It might not be precisely soundproof, but it would not matter to Reynoso, either way.

A torture chamber.

Jumbled images came flooding back to Fowler's mind. A man named Trask from Texas DEA. The leak that Grady Sears and Rudy Stano had been hoping to expose—responsible for Hector Elizalde's death, at least—and Fowler was infuriated by the knowledge he might never have a chance to pass the word along.

From behind him came the sound of footsteps, circling the room. Two pairs of shoes with legs attached intruded on his field of vision. Fowler strained his neck, chin pressed against his chest, to see Reynoso and Dominguez staring down at him, Dominguez leaning on some kind of cane. He could have counted nostril hairs, if he was so inclined.

"You've joined us once again," Reynoso said.

"I thought I'd hang around."

"A sense of humor. Excellent. You'll need it."

"Are you working up a comedy routine?"

"The laugh, as you would say, shall be on you, *señor...*"

"What's in a name?"

Reynoso shrugged. "A minor thing, I grant you, but I feel compelled to find out everything you know."

"Why don't you ask your friend from Texas?"

"As it happens, Trask knew only basic details of your plot. The source—Miami—and the fact that DEA was sending in another man to take up where the late, lamented Hector Elizalde's work was interrupted. I relied on you for confirmation, which you happily supplied."

The irony revived Jack's fading nausea. Reynoso had been gambling on a hunch, no solid way of burning him if Fowler kept his cool. And he had lost it. Blown himself away.

"Well, shit."

Reynoso frowned. "Believe me when I say that I have no desire to cause you further pain. Policemen have their jobs to do, I realize. Of course, you must be killed, but there are many different ways to die. If you are wise and tell me everything you know about your government's attempt to bring me down, I will insure a swift and relatively painless death."

"You're kidding, right?"

"By no means."

"Then, you must be dumber than I gave you credit for. Or maybe you think *I'm* an idiot."

"How so?" A trace of irritation in Reynoso's cultured voice.

"No matter what I say, you have to figure it's a bullshit line to save myself. You'd be a fool to buy it, first time out."

"Your word of honor?"

"In the present circumstances," Fowler said, "it's worth about as much as yours."

The dealer shrugged. "In that case, I must leave you with Jesús. I will return when you are willing to cooperate."

"Don't hold your breath."

Reynoso left them, and Fowler's thoughts were a racing blur as his interrogator made a circuit of the room, examining the target. Psycho-sadism aside, the act of torture could be generally defined in terms of motivation. As a form of punishment, it was a dead-end street, inevitably geared toward termination of the subject with a maximum of suffering, the side effect a lingering example for survivors. Employed in the pursuit of a specific end result—the signing of a false confession, for example—it was useful to practitioners who knew exactly what they wanted and were simply moving toward a preestablished goal. The quest for unknown information was a different problem, though; a riddle for interrogators who were never absolutely sure their subject spoke the plain, unvarnished truth. Some torture victims spilled their guts at once, while others only started talking after hours—or days—of torment. Either way, they might be lying to their captors out of fear, defiance, madness, even eagerness to please.

Reynoso's offer of an easy death had been a standard ploy, designed to start Jack talking, so Dominguez would have something to compare against his other statements later on. It might have worked, if Fowler had not been around this block before.

Dominguez stood in front of him again, and Fowler realized his "walking stick" was actually a wooden sword, the kind employed by martial artists during practice sessions to avoid unsightly accidents. Approximately three feet long and one inch in diameter, it had the look of solid ash or pine.

"We start at the beginning," said Dominguez. "With your name."

"Fuck you."

The trick was not to scream unless you absolutely had to, saving breath and energy for snotty answers that would piss Dominguez off and get him swinging blindly in his anger, rather than selecting special targets for the maximum effect. It worked for all of ten or fifteen minutes, till Jesús caught on and took a breather, coming back refreshed and more determined than before.

"Once more," he said. "From the beginning."

"Joe."

"Your last name?"

"Mama."

"What?"

"Joe Mama, fuckface."

Somewhere in the middle of the second quarter-hour, he began to scream.

MARIA WATCHED the stranger drive away. Another gringo, this one leaving on his own. She glanced across the courtyard, toward John Decker's balcony, and saw no evidence that he had come back to his room.

She had been close to panic when Dominguez interrupted them, convinced Miguel had found her out somehow. Attempting to escape was one thing, but seducing visitors inside the very house they shared would wound his macho pride beyond the point of reconciliation. He would have to kill her, if he knew the truth, and it would not be swift.

Incredibly, she had been spared. Miguel had summoned Decker on some other mission, giving her a chance to dress and sneak back to her room unseen. She cursed the timing of the interruption, catching the American before he climaxed and agreed to help her get away.

She would have won him over, given time . . . but time was running out. If Decker and Miguel were talking business now, it meant the gringo would be leaving soon. Without Maria, if they had not made a deal.

Trusting him was a gamble no matter what he said. She knew enough of men to realize that most of them would lie for sex, professing love, fidelity—whatever was required to get a woman on her back. When they were duly satisfied, the words evaporated like a daydream, lost beyond recall, their solemn pledge dismissed without a second thought.

But Decker might be different.

He was strong, she knew that much, and while he spoke in terms of business coming first, he did not seem to fear Miguel. That was unusual in itself; a solemn confidence, so different from the last American's conceit.

She considered she still had a chance, but a nagging, nameless apprehension stalked the shadows of her mind. Maria shifted nervously and stared at the windows opposite her own. Where *was* he? Were Reynoso's summons and the other gringo linked, somehow? Had something happened to defeat her one more time?

She felt Miguel behind her in the bedroom, smelled the same expensive after-shave that he had been wearing when they met. Maria had been sure to lock her door, but he had passkeys and did not believe in knocking where his woman was concerned. She turned to face him, found him standing by the dresser, studying the contents of her open jewelry box.

A sudden thought struck her. He was not with Decker...

"Miguel."

"I have been careless, *querida.*"

"How?"

He answered with a question of his own. "Have you spent any time alone with the American?"

"You mean John Decker?"

"Sí."

It was a toss-up. She could lie and risk discovery, or tell a version of the truth and shade it to her own advantage.

"Yesterday," she said. "I took a morning swim, and he stopped by the pool house. Why?"

"What did you talk about?"

"I don't remember. Probably the heat. Is something wrong, Miguel?"

"He is a spy of the Americans. The drug enforcement people."

"No."

"Jesús is with him now. It is important that we know what he has learned. If you said anything at all—"

"I don't discuss your trade," she said. "How could I, when you never tell me anything yourself?"

"You still have eyes, *mi corazón*. But never mind. Jesús will find out everything we need to know."

"And then?"

"Do not concern yourself with trifles," he replied. "A lovely woman needs to concentrate on things of beauty. Flowers. Music. Art."

"Of course, Miguel."

He stepped in close and cupped her breast, a gentle lover's touch.

"I wish I could spend some time with you this afternoon, but there is work that must be done. Tonight, perhaps."

"As you desire."

"And what do *you* desire?"

"Miguel—"

"Don't answer. We will speak of this again tonight."

"Tonight, then."

Her mind was spinning as he left her, sorting jumbled bits of information, puzzle pieces taking on a whole new form. If Decker was a federal agent, he must want Reynoso in a cell almost as badly as Maria wanted to be free. They might have something of a common cause!

Jesús is with him now.

Her stomach knotted as the words replayed inside her head. Miguel was not averse to torture, but he often let Dominguez do the dirty work. Jesús enjoyed the dominance, inflicting pain, the power it gave him over other lives. When he was finished with his victims, they were cast aside like rubbish to be burned.

Maria sickened at the thought that she might be too late. The gringo might be dead by now, or injured to the point that he could not assist her. Still, she had to try. Maybe if she was quick enough . . .

The fear rushed in upon her, then, a certain knowledge of her fate if she was captured trying to release a drug enforcement officer Miguel had captured for himself. She could expect no mercy from Jesús, and it would be enough to make Reynoso turn against her finally, for good and all.

And which was worse? A certain death, however painful and prolonged, or the abysmal living hell of slavery she presently endured?

No contest.

For Maria Escobar, the only question left was *how* to help John Decker . . . and herself. It would require some careful thought, strategic planning, but she had no time to waste. She hoped the urgency would override her fear and give her strength, but she would make the effort, either way.

It had occurred to her that she had nothing left to lose.

THE DRIVE BACK to Nogales and the border seemed to last a lifetime. Clinton Trask relied on cruise control and primal instinct for the most part, watching out for cop cars when he passed through towns or villages, wide open on the empty flats where there was nothing visible for miles. A bottle of tequila on the seat beside him kept him going. When he tried to come to grips with a coherent thought, it seemed to wriggle through his hands.

If Trask had been compelled to catalog his dominant emotions, he would certainly have ranked disgust as number one. Disgust with himself, that is; a deep, pervasive loathing for the cowardice he saw reflected in the mirror every time he faced himself.

For openers, his resolution to confront Reynoso had evaporated when he met the dealer one-on-one, then his renewed determination faded when Reynoso sapped the undercover Fed and had him dragged away. Trask didn't know the dead man's name, but he would find out soon enough, when the Miami team came looking for their boy.

And what would happen then?

Play dumb. Act innocent. His cover was intact, and there had been no messages when he checked in with Phoenix several hours back. So far, so good. The odds were it would never click with Grady Sears or anybody else to link his Arizona trip with the assassination of a working agent in Chihuahua. Trask had studied it from every angle, looking for a snag, and he was clear, as far as he could tell.

It would have been a different story had he followed through on his intent to snub Reynoso, tell the dealer they were finished, come what may. Instead of one dead agent in Chihuahua, there would be a matching set, and never mind the subsequent disgrace when DEA's Intelligence Division started picking through the shambles of his life. Trask had no fear of posthumous humiliation, but he *was* afraid to die.

If he was going to confront Reynoso, he would have to deal from strength...and that did not mean facing down a hundred soldiers or whatever number at Reynoso's hideout in the middle of the fucking desert. Later, when he had some time to think and he was safely back in Houston, Trask would find a way to break it off.

Or maybe not.

Whatever happened, he had looked at suicide and found it unacceptable in any form. He might not be a hero, but he always managed to survive...at least so far.

He lifted the tequila bottle to his lips, disturbed to notice how its contents had receded in the past few hours. If it kept evaporating at the present rate, he would be forced to stop for more in Hermosillo, prior to turning north.

No matter.

Trask would do whatever was required, as always. He had not survived this long by taking foolish risks without a safety net. The gambling urge was one thing, where mere money was concerned, but gambling with his life was something else.

His mind flashed on the face of the Miami agent, twisted in a mask of fury as Reynoso dropped his name and Texas DEA affiliation. Poor dumb bastard, thinking Trask had fingered him specifically and playing right into Reynoso's hands with his reaction. If Miguel had not been there, the man would have made a kill, driven as he was.

Terrific. Now he owed Reynoso one, as if the dealer gave a shit about Trask's health or state of mind. If truth be told, Reynoso would have doubtless been amused to watch the captive agent strangle Trask, poetic justice at the bottom line, and maybe something of the sort would be the best for all concerned.

But no such luck.

He tried the radio and lucked in to a channel playing songs in English, in between sporadic bursts of static. Johnny Mellencamp up next, explaining how a person keeps on living, even when the thrill of life is gone.

Trask cursed and turned it off.

Sometime late evening, he would catch a hot bath at his hotel room in Phoenix and relax. It would be over, then, except for dealing with the Monday-morning quarterbacks who picked the pieces up and tried to scope out what went wrong. A few days off, and Trask would be right there to help them, any way he could.

And if the truth got sidetracked...well, it would not be the first time. Close enough for government work, and what the regional director didn't know wouldn't hurt Trask.

As long as he could put the faces out of mind.

The tequila helped, but it was gone now. Cranking down his window, he released the bottle and heard it shatter somewhere in his wake. How far to Hermosillo and a fresh supply?

He tried the radio again and settled on a Spanish tune, got bits and pieces of it through the interference as he drove. The kind of love song Hispanics were forever singing, in between their revolutions and assassinations, when they weren't out running drugs or fighting bulls.

Dear God Almighty, he was tired of Texas and the border, trying hopelessly to close the barn door with a fucking stampede underway. Still, fed up as he was with everything about his job and life in general, Trask knew he would stick it out.

Because he had no choice.

Sometimes, when you were shooting craps, you rolled a natural and raked the money in. Another time you came up snake eyes and were forced to pay. And then there were the *other* times you rolled the dice and never even got to see your score. The dice kept rolling, on and on forever, down a never-ending tunnel, while you ran

along behind and tried to catch them. Knowing, all the
while, that you were too damned slow.

Trask knew the rules, and he had gambled anyway.
Now he had no one he could trust except himself.

And no one else to blame.

13

It had to be the basement. In her four years with Miguel, Maria Escobar had never felt the urge to check things out downstairs, but she was told the basement had been subdivided into several chambers, all of them employed for "storage." No one ever mentioned *what* was stored below, the implication being surplus food, old furniture and janitorial supplies.

But she had not been deaf and blind the past four years. Maria had observed the gunmen trooping up and down those stairs from time to time, Jesús Dominguez often in their company. She listened in on muttered conversations when she could, retrieving bits and pieces that convinced her there was more downstairs than mops and cans of enchilada sauce.

Miguel was famous for the public execution of employees who betrayed him, forcing other members of his staff to stand in tidy rows and watch, but there were other victims he preferred to hide away from prying eyes. Their answers to selected questions were meant for him alone, the screams and tears a private thing.

The basement, then.

Maria had free access to the stairs, but once she got below, she would be forced to seek out her final destination and deal with any guards on hand. A weapon would be necessary, but Miguel allowed her nothing of the sort. Her combs and brushes, lotions and perfumes were useless now. She might seduce a stranger, but the gunmen on Reynoso's payroll knew their lives were hanging in the balance if they violated their employer's trust.

Still, she would need a weapon, and she needed it without delay. It was already growing dark outside. She had delayed this long because she hoped the night would give them cover, if they got that far.

She chose the kitchen out of desperation, knowing time was short. Maria did not cook—Miguel maintained a staff, to leave her free for "other things"—but she was a familiar visitor who joked with the employees and recalled their birthdays, little humanizing touches that endeared her to the rank and file. The chef did not consider it unusual when she dropped in for a chat that evening, sampling the broth and special salad dressing, complimenting each new item in its turn. He did not miss the extra carving knife when she departed moments later, and he would have blamed his kitchen helpers for misplacing it, in any case.

Returning to her suite, Maria tucked the ten-inch blade beneath her pillow, safely out of sight in case Miguel barged in once more. She had an hour and a half until the call to supper, and she meant to use it well. A change of clothes, for traveling: her black designer jeans, a sheer silk blouse to match, a jacket to keep the desert chill at bay. Assuming she would live to breathe the clean night air.

Maria stood before the full-length mirror, dressed for mourning, wondering if there was something she could do about her hair. Utility was more important than appearance now. She opted for a ponytail and used a rubber band to tie it back. Her face seemed pale and wraithlike, but she let it go.

The carving knife went up her left sleeve and nestled there, the point against her flesh, inside the elbow, with the wooden handle covered by her hand. It would not be apparent on a casual inspection, and her target would be momentarily distracted, if she did her job. She left another button open on her blouse as an afterthought, to show more cleavage and attract the eyes.

She didn't find a guard outside the pantry, and she reached the basement stairs without a hitch. A light was burning down below, illuminating walls of cinder block and concrete flooring. New to this domain, Maria had no way of knowing whether it meant guards on duty, or if certain lights were always on downstairs.

Her heart was pounding as she reached the bottom, quickly glancing left and right. Two gunmen at the far end of the hallway, to her left, were engrossed in conversation, with their automatic rifles propped against the wall.

They saw her coming, registered surprise, but neither one of them was visibly alarmed. From twenty feet, she caught them staring at her breasts, a soft blush on the young one's face when he was forced to meet her eyes. The older gunman seemed to be in charge.

"¿Dónde está Señor Reynoso, por favor?"

A glance was exchanged between the soldiers, with the young one shrugging as his partner frowned.

"No sé. El Jefe no está aquí."

Maria made an angry, pouting face and tapped her foot impatiently, the very image of annoyance. Mentally she gauged the distance to their weapons, wondering about the safeties, live rounds in the chamber, calculating whether she could stab one man and reach the guns before his partner cut her down.

On a passing whim, Reynoso had once instructed her in marksmanship, and she recalled the nomenclature for the different weapons commonly displayed around the ranch. These two were AK-47s, noisy and destructive when unleashed on paper silhouettes and empty cans. Their full fury would show when they were turned on human flesh.

She seemed to make her mind up, speaking rapidly as she advanced upon the older gunman. If and when he saw Miguel, she instructed, he should inform *El Jefe* that Maria had grown tired of waiting in her room. If he should ever condescend to keep their date, she might be found outside, and then again...

The gunman tried to interrupt her, begging off, but she was close enough to reach him now. Her right hand found the handle of the carving knife, felt fabric snag and separate as she withdrew the gleaming blade. Momentum took her through the move, a thrust below the gunner's rib cage, each of them astounded by the moment in their different ways. Warm blood gushed against her hand as she retreated, lunging for the rifles.

Stunned, her second adversary made no move to stop her as she reached the AK-47s, scooped one up, and spun to face him with a finger on the trigger. In her excitement she could not remember where the safety was, so she merely squeezed the trigger, hanging on and riding out the recoil as a stream of bullets swept the corridor.

The young man took a burst across the chest, blood spurting as the impact drove him back and down. The older gunman was on his knees and clutching at the knife protruding from his abdomen, his cry of pain cut off as bullets chopped a ragged path across his face. Blood was everywhere, grim images of violent death that barely registered before they were suppressed.

She lifted off the trigger, the echoes of staccato gunfire ringing in her ears. How soundproof were the basement rooms? Offhand Maria could not think of an occasion when she had detected noises from below, but she had never paid attention, and Miguel would not have used the basement for a shooting range. If nothing else, the racket would be audible inside the room the two dead men were guarding.

How much time before a troop of reinforcements came to cut her off?

Maria held the smoking rifle close and started for the door.

THE GUNFIRE CAUGHT Dominguez on the backswing, poised to slam his wooden sword across Fowler's chest, and although the Mexican's face was blurry, upside down and out of focus, it clearly registered surprise and consternation. He was moving toward the door, beyond Jack's line of sight, when it swung open and a woman's voice commanded him to freeze.

Dominguez challenged her, but cautiously, his resistance vaporizing as he learned the guards outside were dead. He dropped the sword upon command and tossed a snubby pistol after it, then knelt in front of Fowler, slightly to the left. He palmed a ring of keys, selecting one to demonstrate before he tossed the whole caboodle across the room. Another order, and he stretched out prone, facedown, hands clasped behind his head.

Chain rattled through a pulley, easing Fowler to the concrete floor. His savior knelt beside him, one hand working on the stubborn cuffs, a rifle pointed at Dominguez where he lay. And it was only then that Fowler recognized Maria, all in black, her face as grim and pale as Death.

She did not ask if he was well; the mottled crazy quilt of welts and bruises on his naked body told the story of his pain. Instead she asked him, "Can you walk?"

He tried, and got it right the second time around. His legs were shaky, still half-numb from lack of circulation, but they bore his weight. He crossed the room with measured strides, a patient coming out of therapy, and reached the weapons that Dominguez had discarded on the floor.

He left the wooden sword and took the pistol, a Smith & Wesson Model 669 in stainless steel. The magazine would hold a dozen round, 9 mm parabellum, and a swift inspection showed him it was full.

The urge to kill Dominguez overwhelmed him, but he fought it down. Instead of squeezing off an easy head shot, Fowler kicked the dealer in his short ribs, stooping as he twisted clear to crack the pistol hard across his skull.

Sweet dreams.

"The hall."

Maria understood and doubled back to watch for reinforcements, covering the hallway with her AK-47 like a seasoned pro. Dominguez was a smaller man than Jack, his slacks unfashionably short when Fowler slipped them on, but they would have to do. The shoes were better, and he skipped the shirt, surprised to find more room inside the dealer's sport coat than he bargained for.

"Let's go."

Two dead men in the corridor, another AK-47 leaning up against the wall. Jack frisked them both for side arms, coming up with a Beretta and a Llama small-frame automatic. Tucking two guns in the waistband of his borrowed slacks, he gave the Llama to Maria, scooping up the surplus automatic rifle.

"Stairs?"

"This way."

He followed her and took the lead when they reached the staircase. Steady pain provided motivation as they climbed, emerging in a pantry, the kitchen sounds and smells close by. He paused a moment, thinking through the necessary moves, aware that any slip from this point on would spell their death.

They needed wheels first thing, before they even tried the gate. On foot they would be run to earth and killed in moments, even if they somehow managed to escape the compound proper. At least with a car their chances would be more than nil.

He grimaced, knowing it was still a long shot, the odds against survival now.

And it was still the only game in town.

They passed the kitchen, moving swiftly, Fowler's legs protesting all the way, but still responding on command. Cool darkness welcomed on the far side of the exit, precious shadows hiding them as Fowler paused and took his bearings.

On their right was the pool house, straight ahead, garages and the vehicles they needed to survive. A splash of light brightened the motor pool, with moths and other insects circling the floods. On Fowler's left, a sentry paced off his route along the elevated catwalk, concentrating on the barren land outside the wall.

It struck him that they needed keys, and Fowler wondered if Reynoso felt secure enough out here to leave them in the cars. Only one way to tell, and if they came up short it would be tough shit all around.

He showed Maria how to hold the rifle down, against her leg, and hide it from the sentry's view in case he glanced their way. A short walk to the lighted island of the motor pool, and they would try their luck. A four-wheel drive if possible, and failing that, the first machine Fowler could obtain.

They reached the vehicles without a hitch, then separated, Fowler checking one row while Maria took the other. There appeared to be no system, some with keys in the ignition, others gone, and Fowler settled on a year-old Bronco, motioning Maria over as he tried the driver's door.

And suddenly it went to hell.

One of the goons in residence emerged from the garage, took one look at Maria with an AK-47 in her hands, and froze. *"¿Qué pasa?"* he demanded, putting force enough behind it to alert the sentry on the wall.

Maria pivoted to face him, squeezing off a burst that punched him backward, flat against the stucco wall, before the piece fell silent in her hands. Jammed or empty, Fowler couldn't tell, and there was no damn time to think it over, as the lookout on the wall began to double back, already shouting the alarm.

Jack brought the captured rifle to his shoulder, aiming quickly, triggering a burst that ripped across his target's legs and spun him off the catwalk, screaming as he fell. Concussive impact cut his voice off with a squawk—no way to tell if he was dead or merely stunned—but there were other gunmen on the way, responding to the call and sounds of gunfire.

Fowler threw himself behind the Bronco's wheel, Maria scrambling in the other side without her rifle, brandishing the Llama automatic.

"Can you use that thing?"

"We'll see."

"Terrific."

Fowler twisted the ignition, praying for a prompt response, and heard the engine fire. He dropped the

Bronco into gear, released the parking brake and stood on the accelerator, fat tires spitting sand and gravel as he took off from a standing start. He found the headlight switch and flicked the high beams on, three gunners suddenly illuminated in the glare. Two of them broke to Fowler's left, the odd man going right, too startled and confused to open fire at once.

For his part, Fowler did not hesitate. The AK-47 was braced across his windowsill and spitting as he passed the guards. He drove left-handed, firing with his right, and saw one man collapse before he left the targets in a drifting cloud of dust. Maria squeezed off two quick shots beside him, and her opposition managed to release a burst of automatic fire, a lucky round impacting on the Bronco's tailgate as they fled.

The gate loomed in front of them, two gunners braced for action, frozen in the high beams, firing from the hip.

"Get down!"

Maria hunched beneath the dash, while Fowler shifted hands and thrust his AK-47 out the window, laying down a screen of cover fire across the Bronco's hood. Incredibly one of his targets staggered, dropping to his knees, the other fading back and covering his own retreat with measured bursts. The AK-47's last three rounds were close enough to make him duck and cover, dropping in a combat crouch.

Jack dropped the empty rifle, bracing both hands on the wheel. The wrought iron gate looked solid, making Fowler hesitate to ram it and risk disabling the vehicle before they even got outside the walls. He hit the brake and fought the skid, the Bronco sliding broadside toward the sentry who had conjured nerve enough to feed his Uzi with a brand-new magazine.

No time to count the shots as Fowler nailed him, firing with a pistol in each hand. The gunner toppled backward, squeezing off a wild burst toward the stars before he fell.

There had to be a switch or button somewhere to control the gate. Jack gambled on the left-hand gate post first and caught a break. One touch and he was making tracks in the direction of the idling Bronco as the gate began to roll on hidden rails.

He smelled the coolant as he reached the vehicle, afraid to stop and check the radiator, knowing there was nothing he could do to patch a bullet hole, in any case. The car was running at the moment, it would have to see them through.

More firing streaked toward them from the center of the compound as he climbed inside the Bronco, slammed the driver's door and raced toward the moving gate. The wrought iron scraped along his side and gouged off strips of paint as Fowler cut it close, then they were through the gap and running over open ground, the gravel one-lane stretching out in front of them as far as he could see.

"Hang on!"

Maria braced herself as Fowler took it off the road and let the Bronco do what it was built for, while they still had power in the mill. A straight run down the single access road would leave them vulnerable to pursuit, while taking to the desert at least offered some slim chance for an escape.

There would be other four-wheel drives around the ranch, of course, but tracking in the dark would still be difficult. Reynoso's people would not know how many guns they had, or how much extra ammunition they were carrying. An ambush in the dark would cost more lives, and while Reynoso would not hesitate to use his men for

cannon fodder, Jack was counting on the troops themselves to drag their feet, self-preservation coming to the
fore.

By morning, if their wheels held out that long and
Fowler managed to avoid the treacherous arroyos, they
would have a decent lead. By then, the hunters who came
after them would make the trek in peril of their lives.

"Is something burning?"

Fowler smelled it, too, but he'd been trying to ignore
the odor when Maria put the question into words.

"They hit our radiator at the gate," he told her.
"We've been losing water since we left the compound,
and we're running hot."

"That's bad?"

"Too hot, we vapor-lock or warp the heads. It's all she
wrote."

"What does it mean, 'Is all she wrote'?"

"It means the engine dies, and we're on foot."

She dropped the subject then, and Fowler made three-
quarters of a mile before the Bronco's engine started
knocking. Still, he pushed the wounded off-road vehicle, determined not to let it die before he made the great-
est distance possible from their pursuers.

Two more miles, and steam was pouring out from underneath the hood, the engine missing, barely holding on.
In front of them, the headlights showed a swathe of
darkness in their path, the brink of an arroyo Fowler
would have had to drive around, if he were driving anywhere.

The Bronco died with twenty yards to go. They coasted
to a halt, and rolling dust caught up with them, a chalky
layer of silt that covered everything.

"Goddamn it!

"So?"

Maria's fear was evident, but she was bearing up. Jack gave her points for trying, knowing he would still be hanging from the parrot's perch—or maybe dead by now—if not for her.

"You saved my life," he said. "I haven't thanked you properly."

"Another time, perhaps."

"Okay."

"What now?"

"They'll spot the car, first thing, unless we hide it."

"Where?"

"Down there."

He pointed to the lip of the arroyo, with Maria catching on at once.

"We push?"

"Unless you've got another engine on you somewhere, yeah. We push."

He set the gears in neutral, threw his weight behind the Bronco with Maria helping, and they rolled it toward the gulley, Fowler cursing at the pain the effort cost him, battered muscles crying out at every heave. Long moments ticked away before he felt the front tires slipping, nosing over into empty space, and then he pulled Maria back as the Bronco disappeared with a clatter in the sandy gorge.

"With any luck," he said, "they'll miss it when the chopper makes a pass first time. If we get *really* lucky, maybe they'll believe we crashed it, and spend some time in the arroyo searching up and down."

Maria nodded, facing him. "What now?" she asked again.

He scanned the dark horizon, watching out for headlights in the south before he turned to face the distant border, hopeless miles away.

"We walk."

14

"Maria *and* the gringo?"

"*Sí, patrón.*"

Miguel Reynoso drew a ragged breath and exercised a major force of will to keep himself from leaping at Dominguez to tear him to pieces where he stood.

In fact, and under different circumstances, Jesús would have made a comic figure, standing in his dress shirt and his empty shoulder holster, nothing but a pair of red bikini briefs and ankle socks below. Reynoso had deliberately refused him time to dress, aware that his condition would humiliate Dominguez further, make him even more receptive to interrogation.

"So, how many dead?"

"Two men downstairs, one of the drivers, and a soldier on the gate. Three other men were badly wounded, *Jefe.* Two of them will surely die."

"I want to know how such a thing can happen in my home, Jesús. I have an army here, and one man makes them look like fools. He makes a fool of *you.*"

"The woman," said Dominguez, stiffening. "She killed the two downstairs and liberated Decker. *She* betrayed you, *Jefe.* I have merely tried to do my job."

"You did not stop her when you had the chance."

"There *was* no chance. The guards outside were shot, and I was going to investigate, when suddenly she's there, a rifle in my face, and there was nothing I could do."

"You could have *killed* her," snapped Reynoso.

"How?" Reynoso challenged. "Those I left outside were armed and ready, but she took their guns away and killed them both. My death would not have slowed her down. I thought the sentries in the yard would pick them off."

"You thought?"

Dominguez risked a shrug. "A woman and a beaten man against fifteen or twenty guns—I had no reason to believe they would escape. And I was knocked unconscious, you recall."

"I'm not forgetting anything, Jesús."

Reynoso paced his study, pausing at the windows facing toward the courtyard. Floodlights burned there now, as if delayed security would somehow compensate for what had gone before. A gunman stood outside the window, glaring at the night, a submachine gun underneath his arm, defending his *patrón* against the insects drawn inevitably to the light.

"They have a vehicle," Reynoso said. It did not come out sounding like a question, but Dominguez answered anyway.

"Ford Bronco, *sí.*"

"And it was hit?"

"We think so. It is difficult so say."

Reynoso was already calculating time and distance, ticking off the odds. They would avoid the major roads, if they were wise, and stick to open desert where they could. That meant a hundred miles to reach the border, if they did not lose their way and start to drive around in circles. Three, four hours at the very least, negotiating dry arroyos and the other pitfalls of the land. Cut that in half if Decker had the nerve to try his luck on Highway 16, picking up the road somewhere between Chihuahua and the Rio Grande.

"I want the highway blocked, this side of Ojinaga. Four men on the highway to Nogales, just in case. You take the rest and run them down before they reach the border."

"*Sí, patrón.*"

"If possible I want them both alive. In any case, Maria."

"*Sí.*"

"Well don't just stand there, idiot!"

Dominguez hurried off to dress and organize his search team, while Reynoso poured himself a stiff shot of tequila and prepared to wait. Say twenty minutes, more or less, before his men were ready for the chase. How far could Decker and Maria travel in that time?

Too far.

Reynoso was not angry at the gringo for escaping. He had ordered the interrogation as a business matter, and he would dispose of Decker when the time came, to protect himself, but he expected no less from an agent of the hated DEA. Maria, on the other hand, had wounded him with treachery, discarding everything he had given her, rejecting him in favor of a narc who meant to bring Reynoso down.

In retrospect it should have come as no surprise, but in his heart Reynoso had believed Maria would accommodate herself to the surroundings, given time. She would accept his love, or a facsimile, and make him proud.

Betrayal by a woman made Reynoso suspect in the eyes of his subordinates. They would begin to question his decisions now unless he proved himself by wreaking vengeance on Maria and the Anglo bastard she had chosen to assist.

He did not know exactly what her punishment should be, not yet, but it would come to him. And she would stand as an example to the faithless *putas* of the world. A lesson in fidelity.

But only if they could track her down in time, before she and Decker reached the Rio Grande, and made connections with the law.

Reynoso poured himself another double shot and gulped it, slouching in his high-backed leather chair and waiting for the night to end.

MARIA HAD WORN FLATS for walking, but the desert still conspired to trip her up and send her sprawling on her face. Sharp rocks and hidden burrows made the footing treacherous, the more so as they scrambled in and out of creek beds etched across the desert's face like open wounds.

She kept her hands free, with the pistol in her belt, and followed the American through the darkness, giving wide berth to cactus patches, spotty scrub and chaparral. Her value as a guide had ended when they left the compound proper, and she knew no more about the endless wasteland than her male companion. He was looking out for rattlesnakes and gila monsters, both nocturnal hunters, but she watched the shadows anyway. A bite might not prove fatal in itself, but it would surely slow the victim down enough that he—or she—would soon be overtaken by Miguel.

The troops would be in full pursuit by now. How many guns? They had disposed of five or six, at least, but there were always more. Reynoso had a never-ending stream of flunkies at his beck and call, including *federales* who might try to head them off before they reached the borderline.

Maria hesitated, wondering if they were even walking in the right direction now. She knew the sun rose in the east and settled in the west, but she had no idea about the moon. If Decker got confused and lost his way, they could be wandering around in circles, doubling back to meet Reynoso's hunting party. They would never know, until it was too late.

She turned full-circle, studying the dark horizon in a search for distant headlights, finding none. It should have reassured her, but the silent darkness seemed to close around Maria like a shroud about to smother her, before the sound of Decker's voice recalled her to herself.

"Maria?"

"I'm all right."

She fell in step behind him, offering a silent prayer that Decker knew where he was going. Even crossing into Texas would not guarantee their safety, but at least he should have contacts there, an agency or network he could summon in emergencies. Strong men with guns, who would protect them from their enemies.

How far was she prepared to go, to win her freedom from Miguel? She had betrayed him, helped his enemy escape, and killed his soldiers in the bargain. It would be enough to sign her own death warrant if Reynoso took her back, but what was left? How would she live in Texas, or wherever she eventually settled?

Would she even be allowed to stay?

Maria had no marketable skills, as such, but there were always training schools. She would be forced to change her name, but Decker might assist with that. His agency might even have a place where she could hide.

And what would she be called upon to do, in payment for her life?

It struck her that she could be called upon to testify against Miguel in open court. The thought of facing him again, regardless of the circumstances, left her sick with fear. She kept on walking, one foot following the other, but her mind began to drift. She saw Reynoso in a cage, but even bars of steel could not contain his evil. With the money and the power he possessed, it would be child's play to procure assassins, even from a prison cell.

Worse yet, her information—gleaned primarily from conversations in the past four years—might not be adequate to build a case in the United States. The murders she was certain of had been done in Mexico, for instance, and the government might send her home to testify.

In which case she was dead.

Maria knew enough about the local law and *federales* in Chihuahua to realize that they would never let her testify. An "accident" or "suicide" in custody would solve the problem well enough, as far as they were concerned. Her legacy would be an item in the daily papers, soon forgotten, and a pauper's churchyard plot without a stone to bear her name.

She brought her thoughts up short. Whatever was required to keep herself alive and free, Maria was prepared to make the sacrifice. If all else failed, at least she had been able to deprive Miguel of something he coveted. His wounded pride would be her victory.

They seemed to walk for hours, though she wore no watch and quickly lost track of time. The landscape never changed, except for dry arroyos here and there, a rocky hill they skirted now and then to save their energy. Fatigue set in around the second hour of their trek, exhaustion creeping up behind and promising to override her fear of capture if Maria gave the feeling half a chance. Although she kept herself in shape with workout tapes, the physical exertion of a night march over rugged, unfamiliar ground was something else, and she was obviously slowing the American down.

"You must go on without me," she informed him, when they finally took five.

"No way."

"They must be after us by now. You have a chance, unless I hold you back."

"You saved my life," he answered, in a tone that brooked no argument. "I'd still be hanging upside down back there, if not for you."

"If we keep walking, it will take at least another day to reach the border."

"Funny thing, I seem to have some spare time on my hands."

"We have no water," she reminded him.

"I got a merit badge in wilderness survival," he replied. "You ever hear of living off the land?"

"You should be wise and leave me here."

"From where I'm standing, it's a sucker bet."

Maria knew it was hopeless, and she let it go. They walked some more, taking five-minute breaks when Decker estimated ninety minutes had elapsed. The last time that Maria checked for trackers, there were tiny points of light on the horizon, but she could not count them accurately or be certain they were vehicles.

No doubt about the passing time, as dawn began to lighten the horizon on her right. On one hand, it confirmed their general direction; on the other, dawn meant they would soon be baking in the desert heat and immediately visible to trackers in the air.

As if he read her mind, John Decker veered in the direction of a stony crag some distance to his left, Maria following behind. He scanned the rugged slope in search of what, she could not say, and found it some time later.

He pointed. "There."

It was merely a dark patch on the hillside, deeper shadow than the rest. Maria frowned. "What is it?"

Decker faced her, smiling.

"Home away from home," he said.

JESÚS DOMINGUEZ SPLIT his task force into teams of four and five men each, four Jeeps' worth, spitting out instructions in a tone that told them any questions would be hazardous to life and limb. A few of them had seen him in the aftermath of the *Americano*'s getaway—his flashy underwear and socks—but none of them was fool enough to laugh out loud. They listened to him with respect, remembering his homicidal temper and their own *amigos* slaughtered by the man they were about to track.

"Señor Reynoso wants the prisoners alive, if possible," Dominguez told his captive audience. "If absolutely necessary, kill the gringo, but the woman must be living when we bring her back." He scanned the solemn faces, almost heard the question in their minds, and said, "She has a special punishment in store."

Some smiled at that, imagining participation in Maria's ultimate debasement, cashing in on idle fantasies. He let them mull the prospect over for a moment, painfully aware of passing time, before he spoke again.

"You each have your assignments, drivers with their compass bearings. Keep in touch by radio and call at once if you make contact. Do not attempt a capture on your own. Remember both of them are armed, perhaps with several weapons each."

No questions as they watched him, fingering their guns, anxious to begin the hunt. Dominguez frowned and nodded.

"*¡Vamos!*"

His trackers broke formation, jogging toward the waiting vehicles. Aside from Jeeps, they had a pair of three-wheeled ATVs at their disposal, capable of checking out the narrow passes and arroyos where a full-size vehicle could never go. The trikes were two-man transportation, with a driver and a gunner riding on the pillion.

Striding to his Jeep, Dominguez took the shotgun seat and nodded to his driver, bracing one hand on the dash as they took off with spitting tires. Beyond the gate, the vehicles fanned out, Dominguez quickly losing sight of those on right and left as they began the search.

No way of telling where their prey had run to in the darkness, but Reynoso wanted action *now,* at any cost. With daylight they could put a helicopter in the air and sweep a broader area, but it was hopeless to refuse Miguel when he was caught up in a rage.

And, to be frank, Dominguez was as hungry for revenge as his employer, fuming at his personal humiliation by the gringo and Reynoso's whore. He would be pleased to kill them both on sight, but it was best to pacify Miguel . . . and taking them alive could have its own rewards. A slow death would be preferable to a simple bullet in the brain, and if Reynoso tired of playing with his captives, then Jesús might get a turn.

Anticipation helped to lift his spirits as they traveled over rocky ground, the driver searching hopelessly for tracks to indicate that another vehicle had passed this way. It might take hours to strike a trail—assuming they ever did—and even then it would be difficult to follow on the dry, unyielding ground.

Still, they were heading in the right direction, if the gringo bastard kept his wits about him and did not become confused. Dominguez knew it would be foolish to pursue the access road beyond a point where they were out of sight from the Reynoso compound, since the local roads would certainly be blocked and heavily patrolled. An open desert crossing was the only hope of reaching Texas now, and even that was hampered by the damage to their vehicle.

Dominguez had observed the signs, where Decker stopped before he shot the sentries on the gate. Dry soil absorbed the leaking water swiftly, but a smell of engine coolant lingered, telling him at least one round had torn the Bronco's radiator, or perhaps a crucial hose. Once they ran dry, the gringo would be stalled by engine failure, forced to make his way across the barren waste on foot.

And they would run him down, eliminate him, if it was the last thing that Dominguez ever did.

He owed the smug *pendejo* that much, anyway.

But mainly Dominguez owed it to himself.

Incredibly, they crossed the trail a quarter of an hour later, slowing as the driver checked it out, confirming tire tracks in a patch of softer ground. The traces disappeared a few yards farther on, but now they had a greater sense of purpose, knowing they were on the trail. Dominguez used his radio to call the others in, converging in a tighter pattern as the search rolled on.

They pulled up short at the arroyo, stopping near the lip, where high beam headlights showed the bank was churned and broken down. Dominguez took a shotgun with him as he left the Jeep and advanced on foot to scan the arid creek bed.

Down below him, lying on its side, the Bronco showed no signs of life. He sent two gunners down to check it out, and covered them in case the gringo had decided this would be the place to make his stand.

In fact, the vehicle had been abandoned. Flashlights, probing the interior, revealed no blood or other signs of damage to the occupants, assuming they had crashed by accident. It was entirely possible, Dominguez thought, that they had ditched the useless car in hopes that it would not be found for hours—even days—while they continued with their flight on foot.

So be it.

To his certain knowledge, they had neither food nor water for the trek, no great supply of ammunition for their several guns. With Decker and the whore on foot, it would be much more difficult—if not impossible—to find their trail, but they would surely keep on toward the Rio Grande and Texas, striving for *El Norte* while their strength remained.

The question was, for how long?

The desert could be merciless, with temperatures above 110 degrees, no shade to speak of on the flats. If Decker angled toward the hills, it would be easier to find a hiding place, but he would add more distance to a hopeless journey, wasting energy beneath a broiling sun.

Dominguez hoped the desert would not finish his prey before he had a chance to do the job himself. He thought of the Italian from New York, his body ripe and bloated like a giant eggplant when they found him, dead for hours. He had been soft, a city boy, but Decker seemed to have more stamina. Conversely, the interrogation would have sapped his strength to some degree, and he might even have internal injuries.

It was a toss-up, then, between the desert and Reynoso's tender mercy. Either way, Dominguez kept his fingers crossed and hoped that he would have a chance to claim his pound of flesh. Ten minutes would suffice, if he could have the gringo bastard to himself. As for the woman . . .

He was smiling as he raised the walkie-talkie to his lips and issued new directions to the far-flung members of his team, convinced that it would be over soon.

As the first gray light of dawn appeared, the hunt rolled on.

15

Fowler had remembered the Italian from New York, and he was careful checking out the cave before he let Maria step inside. The shadows were a problem, as they had no flashlight, but he went in far enough to satisfy himself there were no rattlesnakes in residence. With sunrise directly opposite the rocky slope, he would be able to complete a better search.

For now, it was enough to know that they were covered from an airborne search, as well as from the desert floor below. The cave was visible, of course, but trackers would be forced to climb the hill and check it out on foot—and that would cost them dearly, while the newest occupants had any ammunition left.

As soon as it was light enough, Jack pulled the pistol magazines and checked their loads. The Llama was their weak link, only four rounds left. The Smith & Wesson doubled that, with eight, and the Beretta held eleven. If they were run to earth and cornered, they could hold the cave awhile, but they could not afford to miss.

And they could not hold out much longer without water, either way. He spent another moment taking inventory, pleased to find a key ring in the pocket of his borrowed slacks, a two-inch clasp knife fastened to the ring.

"I'll be right back," he told Maria, and he was on his feet and moving toward the entrance of the cave before she had a chance to stop him.

"Wait!"

''We don't have time. Reynoso will have people in the air already, and I have to track some water down before they get this far.''

He took the Smith & Wesson, leaving her the Llama and Beretta. Fifteen rounds, in case he did not make it back. Outside the cave, he had a preview of the heat to come, then allowed the force of gravity to speed his pace downhill. Jack knew what he was looking for, but whether he would find it was a different matter. Checking the horizon every ten or fifteen seconds, ears cocked for the slightest sound of men and their machines, he ran a zigzag pattern, working outward from the hill for something like a hundred yards, then turning back to sweep another sector as he made his way back to the cave.

In fact, it took him half an hour to find the barrel cactus, half expecting sniper fire at any moment or the chop of rotors as a helicopter gunship swooped to cut him down. Discovering the cactus was a victory, but harvesting the crop gave Fowler pause. Between the gun and penknife, he could find a way to crack the succulent and reach its precious liquid heart, but that would only offer a temporary respite, and it would not slake Maria's thirst. Instead of opening the cactus here, he had to root it up and take the damned thing back intact.

Above all else, he had to do it now, without delay.

He found a wide, flat stone, and used it like a garden trowel to clear a trench around the cactus, digging for its root. When he had gone down several inches and the bulbous plant began to lean, Jack rose and stripped his jacket off, a makeshift shroud to blunt the cactus thorns.

His penknife did the rest, five minutes spent probing, hacking, with his knuckles scraped and bloody by the time he got it done. The sport coat did a half-assed job of shielding Fowler's arms and chest, the long needles working through to score his flesh, but it was worth the pain to buy some extra time.

Maria heard him coming, but she wisely kept her mouth shut, watching over the gun sights as he lumbered into view. He saw the tracks of fresh tears on her cheeks as she came forward, reaching out to help him with the awkward bundle in his arms.

"Watch out for thorns."

"I was afraid you weren't coming back."

"You kidding me?" He forced a smile. "And leave all this?"

It took some time to clip the cactus spines, with Maria helping brace the succulent while Fowler used the penknife. Finally, when they could handle it without a risk of injury, he cut a fist-size plug out of the top, permitting access to the moisture trapped inside. The water tasted odd, but it was wet and almost cool, a blessing after hours spent without a drop to drink. Conserving it, they drank just a little now and wedged the plug back into place, their makeshift water bottle propped up in a corner of the cave.

With daylight, Fowler's first impression of their hideout was confirmed. The cave was relatively shallow, terminating in a dead-end L-shape after twenty feet or so. The hidden chamber in the rear was large enough for two, but only just. In an emergency, they would be out of sight from trackers standing on the threshold of the cave, but concentrated fire would pepper them with ricochets.

Still, it was all they had, and anything was better than the sunbaked open ground outside.

"We'll have to wait for dark before we move again," Jack said.

Maria countered, "Unless they find us first."

"We've got a shot, okay?"

"Okay."

"You must be tired. Why don't you get some sleep?"

She shook her head. "You, first."

"I'm wired. I'll take first watch."

"I couldn't sleep right now," she told him. "Can we talk?"

"All right. We'll have to keep an eye out for our fan club, though."

They scooted closer to the entrance of the cave, a compromise between the rising heat waves and a need to hear the trackers in advance before they got too close.

"I want to know you," said Maria. "You are not the man I thought you were . . . before."

"I do a job."

"It's more than that, I think."

"Sometimes."

"So, tell me."

And he did.

MARIA LISTENED to the gringo's story, from the death of Hector Elizalde to their final bloody moments at the ranch, absorbing everything, immediately grateful for the opportunity to step outside herself and view the problem from a different angle, seeing others in the picture that had previously focused on herself.

She learned his real name—Fowler—and experienced a momentary flash of anger at the thought that somehow he had used her, trying to destroy Miguel, but then the truth struck home. Maria had been using *him*—or trying to, with every tool at her disposal—when her game was interrupted by Miguel. She would have risked this stranger's life to save herself, as she had sacrificed another life before, and only chance or fate had cast her in the role of heroine, releasing Fowler from a trap that would have been his certain death.

She blushed as guilt replaced her momentary anger, but Fowler missed it or chose not to comment as he finished off his story, leaning back against the rough wall of the cave. Outside, a hawk's shrill cry cut through the stillness, echoed once and died away.

"Now you," he said.

"My story is a common one in Mexico," she said. "Sons work the land and carry on their father's name. A daughter is another mouth to feed. If she is pretty, someone's son will marry her and take responsibility for the expense of keeping her alive. Sometimes the family finds another way."

She hesitated, picturing herself in childhood, following her parents to the local mission church, her bare feet dusty from the road. She went to school because the law required it to a certain age, and then no more. She learned the wifely skills—what the professors called "home economics"—from her mother, in a crowded hovel on the outskirts of Piedras Negras. When her older brothers went away to study agriculture and mechanics, she remained at home to cook and clean. Four younger siblings had demanded all her time, until the afternoon she met Miguel Reynoso and her life began to change.

In her imagination she could see the sleek Mercedes limousine, a rooster tail of dust strung out behind it as Reynoso's driver held the pedal down, returning from *El Norte* with his master in the back. It had been market day, Maria bearing homemade beadwork to be sold as souvenirs, a week's work that would earn her forty pesos if the buyer felt especially generous.

She was surprised and frightened when the bright Mercedes stopped, the burly driver climbing out and beckoning for her to cross the road. At first she had refused, but then Reynoso eased his tinted window down and graced her with a picture-perfect smile, his cultivated voice assuring her that he was not a thief of children. He was interested in native art, and when he dropped a thousand pesos in her basket, picking out a single string of beads, Maria stood there speechless, nearly deafened by the pounding of her heart.

"On second thought, I'll take them all," he said. There was more money in the basket than a simple peasant girl had ever seen before. "You shouldn't have to walk so far from home."

Miguel had offered her a ride, and her resistance had evaporated when he told her she could ride up front beside the driver if she liked. Of course, she climbed in back, amazed to find a compact television set and a refrigerator in the car, cold soft drinks sparkling over ice as she was driven home.

Her father had been summoned from the field. The hundred pesos in her youngest brother's fist was enough to bring the old man running, hat in hand. He had his pride, but it was clearly in the girl's best interest to provide a better home environment. She was old enough to marry, with permission from her parents, and a brief delay in the official ceremony was explained as a necessity of business, which required Miguel to leave the country for a time. It would have violated standing law and common decency to sell a child, but if Maria's new fiancée chose to make her family a handsome gift of cash...well, who was being harmed?

There was no wedding, naturally, and Maria understood within a few short months that matrimony did not figure in Reynoso's plans. She served him as a wife, and he was generous enough—beyond her wildest dreams, in fact—but as they passed their first anniversary together, she began to understand her function in Reynoso's world.

Maria was a household ornament, much like the crystal chandeliers and hanging tapestries. She kept Reynoso satisfied in bed, and he displayed her for his guests at social gatherings, dismissing her before they settled down to business. She was free to travel anywhere within the walls of his estate, and sometimes into Ciudad Juarez, with escorts from the rancho. If she wanted female friends, there were the maids to chat with when they had a moment, or the "wives" of visitors who called upon Miguel from time to time.

And by the middle of her second year at the *estancia,* Maria Escobar had learned to hate her life. She came to understand that some of the domestic staff enjoyed more liberty than the supposed lady of the manor. While she could have bought and sold the servants with Reynoso's pocket change, they each had lives outside their work, however humble those might be. Maria, in her turn, had everything she could wish for, short of freedom. From a peasant's life of poverty, she had transformed herself, become a "lady" in a cage.

And in her heart, Maria cursed herself as an expensive whore.

The first time that she tried to run away, one of the soldiers drove her to Chihuahua, foolishly accepting her assurance that the orders came directly from Miguel. It took three hours for the search team to retrieve her, and Miguel had made her watch the soldier's punishment, a savage beating that reduced him to a bloody wreck before her eyes.

The next time she tried it on her own. The guards knew better than to help her, and she waited seven months before she took a car one night and tried to crash the gate. Eight stitches in her scalp was the only visible result, but there were other cuts and bruises—from a whipping by Miguel—that no one else ever saw.

Her third attempt to flee enlisted the Italian from New York.

Her fourth—undoubtedly the last—had brought her to this cave, where Fowler sat and listened quietly, not interrupting her or passing judgment with his eyes.

"He won't forgive me this time," she concluded. "I have shamed him as a man, by choosing someone else. His pride will call for fitting punishment."

"He has to catch us, first."

"Is that a problem?"

"Maybe." Fowler shrugged. "I won't pretend the odds are in our favor, but he hasn't nailed us yet."

"And if he does?"

"We've still got options, limited as they may be. We could surrender..."

"No."

"I don't care much for that one, either," he replied. "The flip side is, we fight it out. Get lucky on a long shot, maybe save a couple rounds in case it falls apart."

"I won't go back," she said. "I can't."

"That makes it easy." Fowler grinned as if he meant it. "We'll just have to kick his ass."

DISCOVERY OF THE BRONCO gave their search direction, but it did not lead Dominguez swiftly to his prey. The desert kept its secrets well, the dry earth hiding tracks, while wind erased them in the sandy patches where a trail might easily be seen. At dawn the helicopter went aloft and flew ahead of them to scout the barren landscape like a hunting dog, but there appeared to be no trace of Decker or Reynoso's whore.

Still, they could not have traveled far on foot, without a highway or the prospect of a lift. They had no map or compass, to his knowledge, and nocturnal hiking in the desert was a hazardous pursuit. Unless the gringo had been studying geography in preparation for his visit to Miguel, he stood a decent chance of getting lost. The woman would be useless as a guide, since her experience outside the compound had been strictly limited to chauffeur-driven outings in Chihuahua, once or twice to Ciudad Juarez.

They *must* be here, and yet . . .

Dominguez dared not go back to the ranch without his prey. He had already been humiliated once; a second failure now would cost his life. If he could not find Decker and the whore, his only hope would be escape across the border, praying that Reynoso would be too absorbed with anger at Maria to begin immediate pursuit.

Dominguez caught himself and frowned. He was not giving up, because he knew the odds and time were on his side. The runners had no food or water, they were hiking over unfamiliar ground, and at least one of them was injured. If they had not been stopped last night, if they had not already lost their way, the sun would quickly sap their strength and leave them helpless as a lizard penned in a terrarium.

It was the helicopter's job to spot them and alert Dominguez, but the radio was silent in his lap. He flicked the switch once, on and off, to see if it was working, and the pilot asked if there was anything he wanted. To cover his embarrassment, Dominguez asked for a report and scowled when it was negative.

He consoled himself that it was still early, with the Jeeps and three-wheel ATVs advancing slowly, running zigzag patterns to insure they did not overlook a hopeful trail. At this rate they could sweep the desert wasteland for a week without encountering their prey... but they could not give up.

The Jeeps were supplied with extra cans of gasoline, which they would share among themselves and ration to the fuel-efficient ATVs. The hunting teams had water, and Reynoso would be trucking food out to a central rendezvous, along with extra fuel, if they had not recovered Decker and the whore by noon.

Dominguez viewed the prospect of a hasty meal beneath the scorching sun with thinly veiled distaste, but he was running out of viable alternatives. A capture was the clear solution, Decker and the whore delivered to Reynoso's doorstep, but the time was creeping up on ten o'clock without a sign since they discovered the abandoned four-wheel drive.

Unwillingly his mind began to scrutinize worst-case scenarios. The gringo might have a hidden radio transmitter or homing device, beaming a signal to guide his friends in a rescue attempt. If there was something hidden in his clothing, they would be directed to Reynoso's ranch instead, but Jesús understood that there were other ways to hide a microchip—inside a hollow tooth or up the ass, for instance, and even underneath the skin.

Jesús reined in his wild imagination, smiling to himself. John Decker was a simple narc, for Christ's sake, not some secret agent from the movies. He was running scared, without direction, hampered by the beating he had taken, saddled with a woman who could only slow him down.

The outcome of the hunt was not in doubt, but it would take some time. The desert seemed to stretch forever, crosshatched with arroyos where a man could duck and hide. The task Dominguez faced was comparable to one ant searching for another on a vacant lot the size of Delaware.

Except that it was twenty ants in search of two, with air support, and they knew Decker's general course, assuming that he had not lost direction in the night. His goal would be the Texas border, an illusion of security in the United States.

But there was no safe haven in the Lone Star State.

Miguel Reynoso's arm could reach across the border, search out his enemies and crush them like worthless insects in the time it took for them to realize their covers had been blown. No sanctuary existed for the traitors who attempted to destroy *El Jefe* on his own home ground.

And no relief for a subordinate who failed in his assignment to retrieve a prisoner. Dominguez knew the price of failure in Reynoso's game, and he was not prepared to fold his hand when he could raise the ante, go for broke and maybe still come out a winner in the end.

The desert sun beat down on everyone without exemption, but Dominguez scarcely felt it now. He had a mission to complete, the stakes no less than life and death. Once you were in the game, it was impossible to walk away. You backed a hunch with everything you had, and if you lost, the vultures dragged you off and someone else was standing by to take your place.

But not today.

Jesús Dominguez was a winner. It would take more than a gringo and a painted whore to bring him down.

He sipped a fat canteen of water, tried the radio again and settled back to wait.

16

Fowler was surprised when no one found the cave that afternoon. He had prepared himself for doomsday, looking forward to a siege with only one potential outcome. It would be *The Wild Bunch* and the Alamo wrapped up in one, a last-ditch stand with twenty-one rounds marked for taking care of business, two for holding back against the threat of being caught alive.

When they were undisturbed at noon, he grudgingly allowed himself a twinge of hope. The helicopter swept past moments later, circling wide and skimming low. The two of them afraid to speak aloud, as if the pilot or his spotter had a hope in hell of picking out their muffled voices, using them as beacons for a strafing run.

The chopper *should* have seen them—seen the cave, at least—and Fowler spent the next two hours listening for Jeeps or dirt bikes, answering Maria's nervous questions with a string of grunts and monosyllables, when he bothered to reply.

After two hours spent lurking in the shadows at the entrance to their hideaway, there was still no sign of hostile movement on the desert floor below. He thought it out, imagining a strike force on the far side of the hill, the scouts already climbing, ready to surprise them from above.

It was enough to make him step outside and check the slope...almost.

By four o'clock he reasoned that the chopper must have missed them somehow. Negligence or misinterpretation of the shadows on the hillside, maybe pure dumb luck. He was prepared to face the fact that even good guys caught a break from time to time.

The cave had sheltered them from some of the oppressive heat, but it was not exactly cool inside. They finished off the water from the barrel cactus by late afternoon, and Fowler sliced off chunks of bitter pulp to chew for moisture, grimacing but making do with what they had.

Official sunset rolled around at half-past six, long shadows stretching out across the desert floor. Outside the cave, it would be light enough to read for another thirty minutes, anyway, and Fowler felt no urge to move while their pursuers stood a decent chance of spotting them first thing.

"Full dark, we leave," he told Maria, heading off her question with a conversational preemptive strike.

"We'll need more water," she reminded him.

"With any luck, we'll find it on the way."

"And food?"

He had ignored the painful rumbling in his stomach during the day, but it would not be still. Maria's had been making sympathetic noises through the afternoon, which Jack pretended not to hear.

"Unless we come across a restaurant out here," he said, "we're out of luck. There might be game around, but we can't risk a shot to give ourselves away, much less a fire. And even if we eat it raw, the hunting takes up too much time and energy. Our top priority, right now, is putting space between Reynoso and ourselves."

"All right."

"Myself, a couple of days of fasting couldn't hurt," he said. "The water's something else, but food won't really count until day three or four."

"And then?"

"By then," he told her, striving for a tone of confidence, "we ought to be across the river, home and dry."

"You think the Rio Grande will stop Miguel?"

"I doubt that he's afraid of water, but I'm counting on a lift or telephone if we find a highway on the other side. Right now he's after us. Throw in the DEA, the FBI, some Texas Rangers, it should slow him down."

"Perhaps."

"Don't give him too much credit."

"I have seen what he can do."

"He's just a man. Connected, sure. He's got a lot of friends and flunkies. But he puts his pants on one leg at a time, just like the rest of us."

She shifted gears and came up with an impish smile. "Is that the way it's done?"

"Except for firemen. They slide down a pole."

"I owe you an apology," she said. "For what I tried . . . before."

"Self-preservation," Fowler said. "We're looking at a different set of rules."

"I was prepared to risk your life."

"You used the tools available to do a job. Don't let it bother you."

But having started the confession process, she could not turn back. "There was another man, some months ago. From New York City."

"I already heard the story from Dominguez," Fowler interrupted her. "One version of it, anyway. The guy you picked on was a heavy dealer, way I heard it. Ask around the Apple, I'd bet money that some cops and parents say they owe you one."

"I saw his body . . . afterward."

"So, think about the lives he ruined and the kids he killed back home. A hundred, do you think? A *thousand?*" Fowler shook his head. "I'd say he got off easy."

"You do not despise me, then?"

"It never crossed my mind."

It was too dark to see if she was crying, but he heard it in her voice. "I'm frightened."

"So am I," he told her honestly. "Reynoso needs to watch his ass. You scare somebody bad enough, it makes them dangerous."

"How long until we go?"

"A little while."

"Please hold me."

Fowler took the lady in his arms and held her close, surprised to feel the stirring in his loins.

"We'll be all right," he told her, wondering if it was true.

"Convince me," said Maria, pulling back a foot or so to face him, sounding breathless as her hands rose to the buttons of her blouse.

"I'll do my best."

MIGUEL REYNOSO LISTENED to Dominguez on the radio, voice fading in and out with distance, trying to explain why there was still no trace of Decker or Maria to be found. Reynoso did not trust himself to touch the radio, afraid he might lose control and smash the set, rip out the microphone and fling it through the nearest window in his rage. Instead he stood beside the operator, waiting patiently until Dominguez finished.

"Tell him to continue with the search," Reynoso said. "On no account may anyone return without the prisoners."

He turned away before the order was repeated, knowing that Jesús would do as he was told. Allowing the American and the woman to escape was bad enough, a capital offense; allowing them to stay at large was worse. Dominguez had one opportunity to save himself and salvage self-respect. If he should fail . . .

Reynoso thought about the consequences, if the gringo and Maria reached the border. Contact with the DEA or FBI, a safe house under guard. He would eventually reach them—no one was invincible—but in the meantime, they would both be filling steno books and reels of tape with information on his private life and business dealings, both in Mexico and the United States.

How many executions had Maria witnessed in the past four years? How many conversations was she privy to, disjointed fragments useless in themselves, providing pieces to a complex puzzle when she placed them in the hands of law enforcement? Decker could supply the details of Emilio Mapache's murder, for a start, and lead investigators to the body if it was not moved in time.

Most of the charges would be tried in Mexico, of course, but it was risky, even so. The government was working overtime to clean its image up and draw more aid from the United States, a process that required some move—however minimal—in the direction of eradicating drugs. Like any other businessman, Reynoso had made enemies along the way, and some of them were still in office. It would please them if he went to prison, opening the field to his competitors while granting them a trophy they could show to the Americans. The sweeping "cleanup" under way.

Reynoso heard the helicopter coming back and realized it must be running short on fuel. He felt an urge to join the search, direct it on his own, but imposition of a new commander in the field would only slow things down, confuse the trackers when it was important that they concentrate. Dominguez was responsible for the escape, and he would pay the price if he could not repair the damage.

Still, if he was honest with himself, Reynoso knew he shared a measure of the blame. He recognized Maria's feelings, even if he could not understand them, and he should have known she had not given up on planning her escape. Her insults in the past had been relatively minor in comparison with this. A beating now and then, to show her who was master, and Reynoso let himself believe she had resigned herself to life at the *estancia*. Maria came when she was called and did as she was told . . . but he should not have let himself believe that all was well.

This time the bitch had gone too far.

Attempting to escape was one thing. He could laugh it off, make sport of her and tell Dominguez she was merely frightened by his amorous demands. A bawdy joke to share with business colleagues over brandy and cigars. It was a different game when blood was spilled, loyal soldiers massacred, a federal agent rescued from the brink of death.

Blood called for blood, and macho honor had its price.

In the event that Decker and Maria managed to escape, against all odds, Reynoso would be calling on his contacts in *El Norte* to reveal their whereabouts and set them up for execution. Clinton Trask would be reluctant to cooperate, but he would play along. His face was known to the imposter now, and if a case was made against Reynoso, they would be together in adjoining cells.

Reynoso reached his study, left the pair of body-guards outside and closed the door behind him. He would be alerted when Dominguez ran their enemies to ground, and he was looking forward to the moment when Maria stood before him, begging for her life. In spite of everything, it seemed a shame that she would have to die.

For honor's sake, Reynoso thought, and steeled himself to make a permanent example of the *puta* and her *Americano*. No one who observed their fate would ever give a second thought to turning on the family, regardless of temptation from outside.

Maria had her uses, even now.

And when he finished with her, after everything was back to normal in his life, Reynoso would go shopping for another fiancée.

Man was not meant to live alone.

THEY WALKED BY MOONLIGHT, silently, alert for lights on the horizon or the sound of engines in the night. By Fowler's estimation, they had covered six or seven miles since nightfall and departure from the cave. It would be creeping up on midnight now, and they had far to go.

Without a map or firm coordinates, he had no way of estimating how much desert lay between Reynoso's compound and the Texas border, but he guessed it must be close to eighty or a hundred miles. A week on foot, if they were lucky and the trackers did not cross their trail, and assuming neither one of them succumbed to heat stroke or exposure in the meantime. If they held the present pace for five or six more nights, without a letup or a careless deviation from their course, they should have reached the Rio Grande.

And then what?

Still more desert, for a start, but they could take a chance on trying highways once they hit the U.S. side. He had no money or credentials, but the pay phones worked on credit for emergencies. If nothing else, they could obtain a ride at gunpoint and explain the circumstances later, after he had been in touch with Grady Sears.

And someone else.

Jack did not know the sellout's name, but he would find out soon enough. The face was branded on his memory, a startled look of fear as Fowler sprang across Reynoso's office, just before the lights went out.

He meant to see that look again, and savor it next time.

Next week was still too far away for Fowler to envision clearly, and he concentrated on the next few hours, taking one step at a time. If it was midnight, give or take, they still had five, six hours' walking time before the sun appeared and set the barren land on fire again. His problem now was where to hide Maria and himself at dawn.

They could not count on finding caves each morning, Fowler knew. That one had been a fluke, and they would have to get along without a stone roof overhead to shield them from the sun. The deep arroyos were a possibility, but they would have to excavate the bank for shade and shelter, which in turn meant hours taken off their walking time . . . if they could do the job at all.

And he could not forget about the water that they needed to survive.

They were not living through a Western movie, where the hero always stumbles on a long-abandoned well or water hole to save him in the nick of time. The early summer had been dry throughout Chihuahua, and the intermittent springs that cropped up here and there around the barren wasteland were exhausted, the creek beds choked with sand and brittle tumbleweeds.

The precious water would be found in barrel cacti and underground, around the roots of hardy plants that managed to survive the heat and drought. Jack pledged to start the search a little earlier this time, while strength remained, and before the morning sun exposed them to their enemies.

He missed the rattlesnake, its warning sound behind him by the time it registered. He turned around to find Maria frozen in her tracks, the diamondback immediately to her left and gliding out between them from the cover of a scraggly yucca plant. Some instinct had permitted her to draw her gun before she froze, but she was trembling as she tried to aim.

"Maria, don't!" he snapped. "Reynoso's people hear that shot, we've got more trouble than a snake."

"Then what?"

"Stand still."

Jack sorted through the information he had stored away the last time he was posted with a raiding party in the Everglades. A snake could strike for roughly half its length . . . or was it just one-third? Whatever, he was certain that the striking distance was reduced for serpents stretched out on the ground, instead of coiled.

As if in answer to his thoughts, the diamondback stopped moving, drawing back into a lazy figure eight.

Poor distance vision, Jack recalled. Pit vipers, like the rattlesnake and cottonmouth, were literally heat-seeking missiles, directing their strike at the body warmth of an intended victim. Rats and gophers were the normal prey, but when a reptile struck in self-defense, most any body heat would do.

Maria's, for example.

Fowler stooped to palm the first large stone he saw, his left hand scooping up a second heartbeat later.

"When I tell you," he instructed, "jump straight back, and try for distance. Make it count. For God's sake don't fall forward."

Edging closer to the diamondback, he scuffed his feet to draw the snake's attention from Maria, knowing it was sensitive to even faint vibrations in the earth. The flat head turned, directed to a point midway between them, and the whirring of the rattles jumped an octave, rising toward a fever pitch.

Jack cocked his arm to make the pitch, and wondered what would happen if he missed...or if Maria slipped and fell. He pushed the image out of mind and concentrated on his target. It might have been a cast-off garden hose, except that it was staring at him, capable of killing Fowler where he stood.

His arm whipped forward, Fowler grunting "Now!" as he released the heavy stone. He did not see Maria's backward leap, for he was concentrating on his aim, intent on scoring one for one.

In fact, he missed the reptile's head and caught it somewhere on the back, along the top curve of its coil. The second stone was off before he had a chance to curse his error, this one aimed better, striking square and hard enough to daze the snake at least.

The rest was nerve and instinct, Fowler leaping in without allowing time to think it through and chicken out. Somehow he found the serpent's thrashing tail and seized it, swung the diamondback around his head and cracked its body like a bullwhip, using force enough to snap the spine and send its severed head caroming through the brush.

"Are you all right?" Maria asked him, coming back, the gun still in her hand.

"Here's breakfast," he informed her. "Leave it on a rock to dry, you've got snake jerky."

"Ugh."

"More food for me, if you pass it up."

"We'll see."

"You didn't hurt a leg or anything?"

"I'm fine," she promised him.

"Okay, let's hit the road," he said. "We've had our break."

Reluctantly she fell in step behind him, keeping pace and following the pale path of the moon.

17

Dawn found them sheltering within a small grove of mesquite and Joshua trees, where Fowler spread his stolen sport coat on the lower branches to provide some shade. That done, he walked around the stand to verify that their hiding place did not stand out on casual inspection, knowing he had done what he could do with the materials at hand.

The grove had not been Fowler's first choice, but it was that or nothing, and he worried that the stunted trees would beckon searchers from afar. Still, the alternative had been a mile or more of open ground in every direction, and they stood no better chance of hiding in a foxhole on the flats, much less surviving the relentless sun.

Snake jerky was not half as bad as he expected, and they washed it down with brackish, muddy water excavated from the soil beneath a thorny Joshua tree. They had enough to live on for the day, but it would be dry walking after dark, and Fowler knew that he would have to find more barrel cacti soon or try to dig himself a deeper well.

Between the trees and makeshift awning, they were fairly sheltered from the sun, the flip side being that their cover cut off much of the prevailing desert breeze. To compensate, they took turns standing on the fringes of the grove to catch a bit of moving air and dry the salty perspiration on their skins.

Jack missed their cave already and hoped they could find a better hideout in the morning, but he caught himself before the fantasy could spread its wings. They might not see another morning, when he thought about it, and his manufactured optimism sure as hell would not make dreams come true.

Last night had been a dream, making love to Maria in the cave before they started hiking out across the flats. He told himself before they started that it was wasting precious energy and sweat, but Fowler didn't give a damn. For all he knew, they might not live another hour—much less five or six more days—and if they lost it, he would have a memory to carry with him when he stepped into the void.

The thought of death brought some men to religion, checking in with long-forgotten deities to beg for favors, making empty promises and bargaining for one more chance. Some others simply gritted their teeth and took things as they came, expecting no more out of life than one more kick while they were down.

Jack Fowler was a fatalist of sorts, but that did not imply he had resigned himself to dying. They still had food and water to sustain themselves for one more day, plus decent weapons to put up a defense if they were found. He thought they had a chance, but only that.

No guarantees.

No guiding beacon from the Man Upstairs to light their way.

He didn't like the odds, but they were not impossible. Some effort, plus a lucky break or two, and they might still survive.

Or they might not.

When it came down to dying, the Chihuahua desert seemed no worse than Brooklyn, the Chicago Loop, or Calle Ocho in Miami. Dead was dead, no matter how you sliced it, and it didn't matter if you went down in a sandstorm or in the winter snow. It all came out the same, with no tomorrow you could count on, nothing but a question mark beyond the last, weak gasp of breath.

He shook himself to break the morbid train of thought, Maria's voice intruding on his reverie. Jack rose and joined her, staring off in a direction he believed to be southeast.

"Right there," she told him, pointing toward a smudge on the horizon, pale and out of focus with the rising waves of heat.

He waited, concentrating on the image, wanting to be sure before he spoke. A moment passed, and then another, with Maria hanging on his arm and waiting anxiously.

"It's dust," he told her, finally, confirming what they both knew. "From Jeeps, whatever."

"Coming closer."

"Yeah, it looks that way."

It was impossible to judge the distance accurately, but he made it something like a mile or two. If they were sweeping as they came, not homing in on the oasis with the pedal to the floor, it could be forty minutes, give or take, before the hunters got this far.

How many?

They would find out soon enough.

"What now?" she asked him, staring into Fowler's eyes as if the final truth were hidden there.

"We either run, or stand and fight. I don't much like our chances running over open ground on a day like this."

"All right."

And it was settled, just like that.

He was amazed the way it really worked sometimes, recalling things you learned in school.

Jack Fowler was remembering the Alamo.

JESÚS DOMINGUEZ KNEW that they were nearing the conclusion of their hunt. It was a feeling in his gut, the moment his binoculars picked out the clump of scraggly trees against the skyline. Two kilometers, approximately, and it seemed to be the only hiding place in sight. If Decker and the bitch had passed this way and come this far, it stood to reason that they must be sheltering beneath the trees.

In any case, it would be worth a closer look.

He thought of calling in the others, finally deciding it would not be necessary. Three men accompanied Dominguez in his Jeep, and one more riding on the ATV that ran ahead of them in search of tracks. The squat tricycle sat beside them now, its motor idling, as the driver wiped his sweaty face and drank from a canteen.

The fewer men involved, the less chance that Reynoso would be disappointed by an accidental death. And greater glory for Dominguez, if he brought the runners in himself, without a full-scale army pitching in.

"Out there," Dominguez told the others, pointing to a dark spot where the trees were barely visible to naked eyes.

"You see them?" asked his driver, sounding optimistic for the first time since the sun had risen on a second day.

"Mesquite," Dominguez said. "A hiding place. We'll check it out."

Behind him, one of the support team offered him a walkie-talkie, but Dominguez shook his head.

"We won't disturb the others yet."

It would have been a simple thing—the wisest thing—to send the helicopter up ahead, but it was bound for the *estancia* to take on fuel. That meant an actual delay of thirty minutes, minimum, between arrival and departure at the ranch, another twenty-five or thirty to return if they were summoned, even in the case of an emergency.

Too long.

Dominguez could explore the small oasis, rule it out or bag their prey, before the chopper was available to help. As for the other Jeeps and ATVs, they would be closer, but he did not feel like sharing.

"Vamos."

In fifteen minutes, they were closing on the stand of trees. Still nothing visible, the scraggly undergrowth permitting only glimpses here and there. The three-wheeled ATV ran in to make a circuit of the grove, its engine noise diminishing around the back side, coming back full-throttle as the trike growled into view.

The scout had drawn no fire, and Dominguez experienced disappointment as his driver slowed for the approach. He had a glimpse of something, in among the thorny trees, but he could not decide if it was furtive movement or a simple shadow, sun-bleached branches shifting in the breeze.

A riot shotgun and an AK-47 stood beside him, wedged between the seats. Dominguez took the automatic rifle, double-checked to verify a live round was in the firing chamber as he stepped down from the Jeep. The ATV was circling back at a snail's pace, trailing chalky dust and taking up position on his right, the driver cradling a submachine gun in his arms. Behind him, three guns in the Jeep were covering the tree line, every eye alert.

Dominguez could have sent a gunman in his place, but he was paying dues, regaining some of the respect Maria and her gringo had destroyed with their escape. Next time one of Reynoso's soldiers told the story of Dominguez, running up and down the compound like a madman in his underwear, some others would recall the afternoon he calmly faced potential death.

The rifle seemed inordinately heavy, hot enough to burn his hands from sitting in the sun for hours while they searched the wasteland. Still, the nagging pain reminded him to stay alert. And he would not have flinched or dropped the gun if it had been on fire.

Some thirty feet before he reached the trees, Dominguez paused. It was incredible how thick the undergrowth appeared. There must be water underneath, deep down, though most of what he saw looked dry and dead, like last year's growth. Sagebrush and tumbleweeds made it impossible for him to pick out solid shapes inside the grove.

"Maria?"

He felt slightly foolish as he stood there, maybe talking to himself. Still, if the gringo and his bitch were listening...

Dominguez took a long step forward, opening his mouth to call again. His eyes picked up a subtle movement in the brush, off center, slightly to his left, and he was turning with the AK-47 when a shot rang out. Dominguez saw a puff of dust or smoke and felt the bullet strike his rib cage with the impact of a hammer stroke.

The world exploded. He was conscious of his finger clenching on the AK-47's trigger, spraying bullets in a careless arc at least six feet above his target as he toppled backward in the dust. More firing from the Jeep and ATV, with swift return fire from the trees.

You never hear the shot that kills you.

It was "expert" information, shared by fighting men for generations, from the Argonne forest to the Mekong

Delta and the streets of Ciudad Juarez. A bit of sage advice, presumably designed to pacify a novice under fire.

And in his final moments of awareness, tasting blood and feeling dead inside, Dominguez knew it was a lie.

THE FIRST SHOT TOOK Dominguez down, his AK-47 spitting high and wide as Fowler shifted, tracking to his left with the Beretta, toward the gunner on the ATV. No way of knowing if Jesús was down for good, but it had been a solid body shot from twenty-something feet, and Fowler needed every round he had to try and clear the decks.

Away on Fowler's right, Maria opened up on cue, the Llama burning up its last four rounds in rapid fire. Too fast. Instead of checking out her aim, the way he wanted to, Jack went about his business, sighting on the driver of the ATV.

The guy was standing, straddling his trike and blasting with an Uzi braced against his hip. The bullets came in twelve or fifteen inches over Fowler's head and showered him with dust, obscuring his target, but he had it locked and he squeezed off two rounds anyway, the killer instinct taking over as he fired.

Dust cleared, and he caught the last part of his target's backward somersault, feet kicking as the gunner did some crazy break dance in the sand. The ATV blocked Fowler's view, and he was not about to waste another round on spec, not before he dealt with the surviving shooters in the Jeep.

He turned, eight rounds in the Beretta and an equal number in the Smith & Wesson at his side. The Jeep was moving, creeping forward with a dead or wounded man behind the wheel. One of the riflemen was crouched behind it, using it for cover, waddling along and cursing to himself in Spanish as the vehicle kept inching forward, threatening to leave him in the clear. He popped up now and then to fire a burst along the tree line, but he did not seem to have a target singled out.

The other heavy was in motion, breaking in the opposite direction, squeezing off one-handed a long burst from his M-16 as he ran. His other hand was wrapped around a walkie-talkie, pressed against his face and shouting something that could only be a call for help.

Jack led him by a fraction, squeezing off a round to find the range, then three more for effect. The gunner stumbled, dropped his radio and went down on his knees, one hand thrown out to brace himself and keep from falling on his face. The M-16 spat half a dozen rounds in Fowler's general direction, whipping up a minor dust storm as he aimed and fired again.

Third time worked like a charm, the shooter choking on a round that bored in underneath his chin and pitched him over on his back.

Four down, and one to go.

Fed up with hide-and-seek, the man behind the Jeep ran out in front of it, ten feet or so, and held the trigger of his automatic rifle down. His grip was solid, and he kept on firing after Fowler shot him in the face, the weapon's recoil spinning him around and backward as the last rounds from his magazine ripped through the Jeep.

The engine stuttered, choked and died. Steam leaked out from underneath the hood as Fowler stepped from cover, closing with the Smith & Wesson ready in his hand. He checked the bodies one by one and found the driver on the ATV still breathing when he got there and retrieved the Uzi, along with a pair of extra magazines.

Jack did not feel like shooting him again, and left him there to work it out while he went on to check the rest.

All dead, Dominguez staring blankly at the washed-out sky, his wheelman drilled by two of four shots from Maria's pistol. Crumpled in the dirt, the shotgun riders were beyond resisting as he stripped them of their arms and extra magazines.

"It's done," he told Maria, feeling her behind him as he made a rapid inventory of their arsenal. Two AK-47s and an M-16, the Uzi and a riot shotgun from the Jeep, assorted side arms lifted from the dead. Jack wanted all of it, but there was too damned much to carry. He selected two Berettas from among the handguns, for compatibility of magazines, and pitched the others back among the trees. One of the AK-47s joined them, but he kept all seven of the loaded magazines, together with the Uzi, riot gun and M-16.

Whatever happened in the next few hours, they would not go down without a fight.

"Jeep's had it," he informed Maria, moving to inspect the ATV. It looked undamaged, and there was room for two on board. No fuel gauge, but he fetched a gas can from the Jeep and topped it off, reluctantly abandoning the extra gasoline.

"Let's see what else they brought us."

In the Jeep he came across a canteen and a water bag. He checked them both and poured the canteen's contents in the bag to simplify their load. They had too much to carry as it was, but water would be crucial with the wasteland still ahead.

"He warned the others," said Maria, nodding toward the dead man and his silent radio.

"We've still got time," Jack told her, striving for a tone of confidence he didn't feel. "We'd hear them coming otherwise."

He stripped the Smith & Wesson's magazine, extracted the 9 mm rounds and slipped them in a pocket of his sport coat. Handing one of the Berettas to Maria, with some extra magazines, he tucked the other in his belt, adjusting it for comfort and convenience. Next the Uzi went around his neck, the strap adjusted so it hung around waist level in the front. Four magazines weighed down his jacket on the left, with spare clips for the AK-47 adding balance on the other side.

"You'll have to carry these," he told her, pointing to the rifles and the riot gun. "Okay?"

She nodded, and Fowler helped as she slipped on bandoliers of ammunition, looking rather like the female lead from some exotic Pancho Villa movie with the weapons in her arms. They walked back to the waiting ATV, and Fowler settled in the driver's seat.

"Hop on."

She took the pillion, the long guns wedged between them, with her arms around his waist. Without the touch, the hardware pressed against his spine, Jack would have thought he was alone.

The driver of the ATV had given up by now, his chest no longer moving underneath the bloodied jumpsuit. Fowler revved the engine, taking a moment to become familiar with the vehicle before he eased it into gear. The sun's position told him he was headed in the right direction as he started north.

It took a mile or two for them to feel entirely comfortable with the ATV. They were not making any record speeds, but they were moving, and it damn sure beat an endless trek on foot. Reynoso's men would home in on the radio distress call, spend some time at the oasis with the dead, before they got their act together and resumed an organized pursuit.

How long?

He had no way of knowing, but the odds had shifted slightly toward the underdogs. They were not free and clear by any means, but they had picked up water, weapons and a means of transportation that should see them to the border if they were not overtaken on the way.

And if they were?

Jack closed his mind to the alternative. If they were intercepted, they would fight. They had no choice, and he had come too far to contemplate surrender now.

A game like this, you bet it all and let the winnings ride. You fucking went for broke.

The sports announcers called it sudden death, and they were right, at that.

18

The radio alert came through at half-past one, a contact to the north, and they were airborne thirteen minutes later. Dressed to kill, a pistol on his hip and automatic rifle gripped between his knees, Miguel Reynoso scanned the barren desert floor and kept his fingers crossed that they would be in time.

The message had been somewhat breathless, laced with interference, but his pilot understood the general directions well enough to put them in the ballpark, keeping up a running dialogue with spotters on the ground, correcting as he came in range and squelched the static. Up ahead the small mesquite grove was a blot on the horizon, like the dark spot on an X ray that foretells disaster.

"Circle once before you land," Reynoso ordered, peering at the vehicles and tiny figures on the ground. He noted several prostrate bodies, did not bother counting them, as numbers had no consequence. His soldiers were expendable, replacements breeding endlessly in Ciudad Juarez, Nogales and a dozen other border towns.

"It's clear," the pilot told him, verifying his assessment as the helicopter hovered, settling in a cloud of dust that made the trackers turn away and shield their eyes.

Reynoso took his rifle with him as he left the whirlybird, the midday heat assaulting him and wringing perspiration from his pores. He scanned the row of anxious faces for Dominguez, frowning as a gunner named Cardoza met him on his way to the circled Jeeps.

"What happened here?"

Cardoza frowned. "We think Señor Dominguez found the prisoners."

"You *think?*"

"One of his soldiers called for help, *patrón*. They were already under fire. He did not give us clear directions, but we had a general idea of where they were."

"Jesús?"

"All dead," Cardoza told him. "Guns are missing, and a motorcycle."

Pushing past his idle troops, Reynoso found Dominguez stretched out on the ground, his eyes locked open in a sightless stare. The blood that soaked his shirt had crusted over and was drawing flies.

Reynoso counted bodies, writing off the five and concentrating on the missing ATV. "How long?" he snapped.

Cardoza checked his watch. "Since the alert, almost an hour, *Jefe.*"

Damn! They would be rolling north at ten or fifteen miles an hour minimum—or faster if the gringo had experience with off-road vehicles. An hour's lead would place them nearly halfway to the border from their starting point, unless the washed-out creek beds and arroyos slowed them down.

Reynoso felt a sudden rush of dizziness, entirely unrelated to the heat. He saw his plan unraveling before his eyes and knew that he would have to act without delay to salvage it, prevent Maria and the gringo from connecting with the DEA across the Rio Grande.

He had a sudden thought and turned to face Cardoza. "Did they take the radio?"

"No, *Jefe*. Just the guns and ATV."

Small favors. For whatever reason, Decker had not seized the walkie-talkie, thereby giving up a chance to call for help before he found a telephone somewhere across the Rio Grande. It might be all the edge Reynoso needed if he acted soon enough.

"Go after them!" he shouted, pointing north as he retreated to the whirlybird.

Cardoza was keeping pace with him and tugging at his sleeve. "Señor Dominguez and the rest?"

"We have no time," Reynoso told him, feeling like a parent with a backward child. "Come back for them when it is finished."

"Sí, patrón." Cardoza did not like it, but the man would do as he was told.

Each one of them would, when it came to that. They might have friends among the dead but none of the survivors would incur Reynoso's wrath by flagrant disobedience.

He reached the helicopter, hauled himself into the empty seat and started giving orders as he grappled with his safety harness. They were in the air a moment later, whipping sand up in the faces of his soldiers on the ground. They left the Jeeps and ATVs behind, Reynoso confident that they would follow in his wake without delay.

Somewhere ahead of him, Maria and her gringo would be fanning sparks of hope into a timid flame. Miguel could picture them, the first time since they ditched the Bronco that they dared to cherish any optimism. Still outnumbered, miles to go, but they were making progress.

Would they feel Death coming up behind them, breathing down their necks? The mental image made Reynoso smile. He rode the death wind, following his

human targets like a guided missile, homing on the scent
of fear.

They might not feel him coming yet, but they would
see him soon enough.

And by the time they recognized him, it would be too
late.

IT WAS EXHILARATING, riding on the back seat of the
three-wheeled bike. Their speed was not exceptional, but
riding in the open, with the desert wind around her, made
it feel like more than twenty-five or thirty miles per
hour—and at least Maria had a sense of doing something, going somewhere.

Going *anywhere* was an improvement over standing
still, and she had come to trust Jack Fowler with her life.
The odds were still against them, but they had a fighting
chance.

And she would go down fighting, if it came to that.

Maria knew they must be closer to the border, thirty
miles or less by now, if they were still on course. It had
been easier to tell when they were walking, slow enough
to check the sun or moon at frequent intervals and make
corrections in their course. Still, she preferred their present mode of transportation, relishing the breeze and the
security of military hardware resting in her lap.

For every gun they had, of course, Reynoso's people
would have five or six. No matter. When they finished
picking over the remains of his lieutenant and the others
back at the oasis, their pursuers would proceed with
caution, knowing they were up against a ruthless enemy.
The hunted animal had shown its teeth, drawn blood, and
the remaining searchers would have images of death in
mind as they resumed the chase.

With no muffler on the engine, the ATV was loud enough that she almost missed the helicopter, did not hear its rotors chopping overhead. The first suggestion, when a vast insectile shadow fell across them, brought her head around, and she warned Jack Fowler they had been discovered. Sweeping past them in a low, wide turn, the chopper came back with someone leaning out the open door and firing at them, bullets spouting dust along her flank before the sounds of gunfire reached her ears.

She did not recognize the gunman, had no time to register his features as the helicopter swept across their path, dust swirling from the rotor wash. Maria clutched the precious guns and water bag as Fowler swung the ATV off course, the fat tires jolting over rugged ground. He turned and shouted something to her, but all of it except the word "arroyo" whipped away.

Ahead of them was a sudden slope. Maria gasped and caught a handful of his jacket as the ATV nosed over in a dive. Around her, sandy cliffs blurred past, a churning cloud of dust thrown up behind them as a beacon for the hunter overhead.

Jack nearly killed the engine as they struck the bottom of the wash, downshifting just in time to save it, managing another burst of speed before the helicopter's shadow blotted out the sky. Some thirty feet ahead was a sharp left turn with overhanging walls, before the gully opened out again.

"Hang on!" Jack shouted, dragging on the handlebars to make the turn and nosing in against the bank. "Okay, stand clear!"

He helped her with the weapons and the water bag, the gunship hovering above them, momentarily prevented from a killing shot. Maria squirmed beneath the bank and dragged her cargo after her as Fowler swung his submachine gun up and fired a long burst overhead. Spent cartridges were scattered in the dust, and while she could not tell if any of the rounds struck home, the helicopter veered away and out of range.

He came back, reaching for the AK-47, and she let it go.

"We haven't got much time. I'll try and draw them off," he told her, glancing up the wash in the direction they were headed when he stopped the ATV. "I may get lucky."

He was gone before she had a chance to speak, and she lost sight of him a heartbeat later. Then her ears filled with the chopping sound of rotors overhead, and Maria cringed for a moment before finally making up her mind.

The ATV was heavy, awkward, and she was not certain she could drive it even if she got the engine started. Still she was driven by the need to do something to distract the airborne gunners, and she had to do it now, before Jack Fowler threw his life away.

She chose the M-16, uncomfortable with the shotgun's weight and the recollections of a similar weapon's painful recoil during one of Miguel's little practice sessions. The magazine was nearly full, and there were several extras in the bandolier she wore across her chest.

A blast of automatic fire released her frozen muscles, sand and gravel slipping underneath her feet as she began to run back toward the open mouth of the arroyo and the slope where they had entered, torn and scarred by knobby tires.

She reached the flats, the bright sunshine nearly blinding her, and hesitated for a moment, scanning for the enemy. Its sound directed her, the helicopter circling over the arroyo some hundred yards away, the gunner stroking short bursts toward an unseen target on the floor of the ravine.

Toward Jack.

She checked the safety on the M-16, made certain it was off, and sprinted toward the helicopter, firing as she ran.

THEY HAD a momentary standoff going, but Fowler knew it could not last. The gunship had to be in contact with pursuers on the ground, and every moment Fowler wasted dodging in and out of view would only put them that much closer to the kill.

How many trackers left?

He knew of five that would not be among the final number, but he counted on Reynoso pulling out the stops to bring him down. They still had hope, however slim, but he would have to take the chopper out, eliminate Reynoso's airborne eyes, before they had another chance to run.

To that end, Fowler showed himself deliberately, inviting hostile fire and answering with short bursts from his captured AK-47. It was on the sixth or seventh pass, a dark face staring at him over gun sights, when he recognized the shooter in the whirlybird.

Reynoso.

Christ almighty, he had come to do the job himself. The macho thing in action, saving face.

Jack's mind switched into overdrive, remembering a hundred different Westerns where an Indian attack was foiled by someone picking off the chief. Reynoso and his shooters weren't Apache braves, by any means, but it was still an angle to explore. Dominguez was dead already, wiping out the second in command, and if he cut the serpent's head off there was bound to be a lull of sorts, at least some lag time while the others argued over who was next in line.

The shock of recognition and the stream of consciousness that followed almost got him killed as Reynoso squeezed off a burst of automatic fire that sprayed his face with stinging sand and gravel. Fowler danced away, returning a burst and knowing that he had not aimed it well enough, before he ducked back under cover, dodging for his life.

The rifle's magazine was almost empty, and he ditched it, feeding in a fresh one from the canvas bandolier around his neck. The Uzi was a dead weight on his chest, and Jack reloaded it, as well. A backup, just in case.

The only way to play it—and to nail Reynoso—was by giving him a target he was bound to try for, going one-on-one against the dealer's clear edge in mobility. He let the chopper make another pass, no firing this time, as Reynoso saved his ammo for the kill.

Jack broke from cover in the helicopter's shadow, lining up a quick burst at the tail rotor, apparently missing as the gunship banked into its turn without a hitch. It circled back for the kill, a jousting match so damned one-sided Fowler almost laughed aloud.

Until he heard the sound of gunfire, coming from his right.

He cast a glance in that direction, cursing as he wondered how the ground team could have come so far, so fast. The anger blurred into anguish as he recognized Maria with the M-16, advancing on the run and firing measured bursts as she came on.

The pilot saw her first, and there was no telling whether she had scored a random hit or not to make him notice her. From where he stood, Jack saw the pilot gesture, pointing out the woman to Reynoso. And he did not have to guess the dealer's orders, as the gunship swung around and went to meet her.

Fowler loosed an angry burst from where he stood—too far to be effective—and the chopper met Maria half a football field away from where he stood. She held her ground, unflinching, emptying the M-16 as spouts of sand raced toward her, following the pattern of Reynoso's grazing fire. The first hits were on her legs, and then the rest of it, too fast for Fowler's mind to cope with as she shuddered, shook, began to come apart before his eyes.

Reynoso, happy with the entrée, ordered the helicopter back around to find a suitable dessert. Jack tugged the Uzi off its sling and gripped it in his left hand, AK-47 balanced in his right and braced against his hip.

"Okay, Slick. Come and get it."

The gunship hovered a moment while Reynoso changed his magazine, and then the beast nosed down, advancing in a rush, the rotor wash propelling grit and sand before it in the pattern of a fan.

Jack's eyes were narrowed down to slits as he stood and gauged the distance, firing with the Russian automatic rifle at a range of thirty yards, the Uzi kicking in a heartbeat later. Waiting for the last split second, when he threw himself aside, an awkward, dusty roll, and came up firing at the underbelly of the aircraft, pelting it with everything he had.

A plume of smoke rewarded him, and then another, indicating something wrong with the controls as it began to pitch and yaw across the washed-out sky. The pilot—or Reynoso—had enough control to make the circle, coming back, and Fowler had a fresh clip in the AK-47 by the time the chopper wobbled onto course, smoke streaming from the damaged fuselage as it began the final pass.

He used both hands to aim this time, the dark faces in the cockpit serving as his target. Holding down the trigger and correcting slightly in the two, three seconds that it took to empty out the rifle's magazine.

He had a quick glimpse of Reynoso, slumped back in his harness, with the rifle trailing in his hand, before the pilot lost it, dead hand fumbling the controls and going for a barrel roll.

They didn't make it.

Fire and thunder erupted in the middle of the wasteland, with the chopper coming down inverted, rotors whipping at or near the same spot where Maria lay, before the fuel tanks blew. The shock wave ruffled Fowler's hair and clothes.

It was the sudden flash of heat, he told himself, that brought the moisture to his eyes.

No time for celebration as he dropped the Uzi, kept the AK-47 with him, pounding back through the arroyo to the waiting ATV. He kept the water bag and ditched the other weapons, got the engine started on his second try, and ran the three-wheeled dirt bike back in the direction he had come from.

He made himself go past the smoky funeral pyre that marked Maria's final resting place, Reynoso in there with her, somewhere in the flames.

As Fowler reached the level ground, he picked up distant engine noises, turned and saw two Jeeps approaching, with another ATV positioned on their flank. The tiny caravan pulled up at sight of the demolished helicopter, armed men staring at the twisted wreckage, then at Fowler, back again to try and penetrate the flames.

He left them to it, rolling north across the flats before one of them had a chance to change his mind. The border was somewhere up ahead, still waiting for him if he ever got that far.

And if he didn't ... what the hell?

Jack Fowler cranked up the accelerator, slouched back in his seat and let the hot wind whip his thoughts away.

19

The Houston Federal Building filled a block between Smith Street and Brazos, with a fair view of Sam Houston College on the west. Some days, in spring and summer, you could stand behind the tinted windows—anywhere above the seventh floor—and scan the open campus with binoculars, in search of coeds kicking back in halter tops and clingy shorts. Come fall, it would be sweaters, showing less, but promising a great deal more.

That morning, as he left his federal four-door in the underground facility, young women were the last thing on the mind of Clinton Trask. A pair of IRS types shared the elevator with him, up as far as five, their conversation full of liens and debits that were gibberish to Trask, and doubtless grief to some poor bastard on the street.

Alone from five to nine, he concentrated on the news flash from Chihuahua that had brought him home two days ahead of schedule, cutting short his leave so he could stay on top of the Reynoso break and see if he could seek out any solid indication of a link at DEA.

There was suspicion, sure as hell; no way around it, after Elizalde bit the big one and their boy on the job went down in flames. But Jesus, the Miami ringer went and took Reynoso with him, like some kind of fucking Wild West show. It simply wasn't the way the game was supposed to be played, and Trask found himself strung out from wondering if there was any game to save.

He had to think Reynoso would be too smart for a diary, any kind of crazy shit like that. A peon who had come up from the streets, he knew enough to keep his thoughts inside, write nothing down if it could ever be employed against him by the law or other enemies.

Dominguez was dead, along with something like a dozen others, from the first reports, and that meant fractured continuity. Could be a blessing in disguise, Trask thought, if everyone who knew of his involvement with the family went up in smoke. The money would be tight awhile, without Reynoso's envelope to count on every month, but he had salted some away for rainy days.

And he could hear the distant thunder now.

There was one advantage about a clean sweep; it would leave him free to choose, if he should ever be approached again. A chance to do it right, next time, and maybe keep his hands clean if he didn't need the money that badly.

Trask had always wondered what it felt like, being born again, and now he had the glimmering of an idea. It meant having his clumsy sins wiped away, and with any kind of luck, starting from scratch, maybe this time not fucking it up so badly.

And if his monthly paycheck still felt light, there would be ways to make a new connection on his own initiative. Approach the sleazy bastards with an air of dignity and quiet strength, to let them know first thing he was in charge. No comebacks later on, where they were threatening to spill the beans and trash a twenty-year investment of his time.

It startled Trask to find that he was thinking of a new relationship with dealers this soon after the Reynoso flameout. Still, it never hurt to keep his eyes and options open in a world where killer deals were made or lost within the time it took to shake a hand or nod his head.

There would be ample opportunities, if Trask went looking for them, but he had to let the heat die down awhile before he started shopping for a new connection in the south. Find out who took Reynoso's place, for openers, and if it was not someone he could work with comfortably, Trask could think about a different merger, helping some young turk with courage and intelligence to move up the ladder in a hurry.

Or, if he got tired of playing both ends off against the middle, he could always pull the pin. Retire, damn right, and start to tap the secret bank account he had established in the Cayman Islands. Morosely he adjusted his collar, thinking that there was nothing wrong with taking off and spending cash while he was young enough to get some benefit, before the fucking doctors started bleeding him.

An early out would cut his pension back substantially, but Trask could more than make up for the difference from his private stash. No taxes on Reynoso's money, either, if he spent it wisely and didn't go overboard with a new Mercedes or a yacht, some crazy shit like that. As long as he paid reasonable taxes on the money they could see, the vampires out of IRS were happier than pigs in shit. Conversely, if they saw money that could not be explained...well, then it wasn't *them* in trouble, and no one came out happy but the government.

His secretary met Trask with a cheery smile. A message waited on his desk from Grady Sears, upstairs, to come around and talk ASAP. About Reynoso, Trask decided, dreading it and knowing there was no way out. He was supposed to know about the case, and there was no damned reason in the world to think his cover had been blown. There had been no calls or telegrams to Arizona, and he'd checked in regularly with the office, even if he had to call them once from the Reynoso hardsite down in Mexico.

Trask wasn't clean, but he was covered.

At least, he thought he was, until he walked into his private office, closed the door behind him, turning toward his desk to sort some notes before he met with Grady Sears.

And found the fucking ringer from Miami waiting for him, kicked back in his leather chair, with feet propped on the corner of his desk.

Alive and well. Some sunburn, sure, but otherwise...

"You'd better have a seat," the ringer told him, putting on a crooked grin. "You look like you've just seen a ghost."

JACK SAW the look of recognition, noted it, and watched the sellout's world come crashing down. His shoulders sagged, arms hanging limp at either side, before he caught himself and tried to put some military ramrod in his spine. He nearly made it, but the effort cost him, and he hobbled to an empty chair across from Fowler, facing toward the desk.

"Surprised?"

"You might say that."

"Your buddy had a little accident."

"I heard."

"That leaves us with a problem."

"I suppose it does." The deputy director's voice was flat, a lifeless monotone.

"I'd like to know what pushed you over."

"What's the difference, now?"

"Let's call it simple curiosity."

Trask shrugged. "You wake up one day and you're forty, forty-five years old. How old are you?"

"I'm getting there."

"Okay. You look around, and suddenly it hits you—you've been working all your goddamned life... for what? Four rooms you live in, and a desk downtown. Three weeks' vacation every year, if you can put your hands on scratch enough to go someplace and sit around a cheap motel."

"You sold out to Reynoso for a mid-life crisis?"

"Call it what you want. I like to gamble, and I mostly lose. Shit happens."

"What I see is that when you're around it mostly happens to the other guy. Like Hector Elizalde, for example."

The deputy director tried to smile and settled for a bitter grimace.

"You're telling me I should have done the manly thing. Fess up and take the heat, instead of selling out a brother."

"More or less."

"I hope you're never in a place you have to make the choice. Since I'm a betting man, let's put my money down on number one."

"That simple."

"It was never simple," Trask replied. "You want to hear that I'm allergic to the mirror lately—fine, I am. If that helps you sort things out, I'm happy for you. Judging someone's always easier than wading through the shit yourself."

"I've been on the receiving end of your solution to the problem," Fowler said, stone cold. "Don't hold your breath for sympathy."

Trask lifted his shoulders in another listless shrug. "What happens now? You talk to Sears?"

"We've met."

"My testimony won't be worth a shit. I always dealt directly with Dominguez or the man. Sometimes a phone call, voice I didn't recognize. Go here, go there, call such-and-such a number in an hour. Cloak-and-dagger shit. There's no one left to prosecute."

"No one but you."

"I don't know if Reynoso told you, but I didn't know you, going in. He faked you out."

"I think he mentioned it."

"I thought you had me, even so."

"And now I do."

"What's Grady want?"

"He's leaving it to me."

"A show trial gets the headlines, but it also has a downside. People see a cleanup going on, they never thank the janitor. Too busy asking how the place got dirty, and can we be sure we really got it all."

"So, what's the answer?"

Fowler was startled by the hollow sound of laughter from the man across the desk.

"If I knew that," Trask said, "we wouldn't be here."

"Well, you're looking at conspiracy and misprision—neglect of duty, wrong performance—to start. Accessory before the fact to murder of a federal officer. The bribery thing's a separate deal, and there's the IRS to deal with. I suppose you stashed the money out of country?"

A barely visible nod from Trask confirmed the supposition.

"Well, you've got laws on currency to deal with, then. It's running into time and money, right? You have to figure that once they've got you, if they can't get anybody else, they go for the example. Throw the book and then some. Maybe dig up laws you don't remember from your days at Louisiana State University."

"You read my jacket?"

"Making sure. The photos were enough, but I like knowing who I'm dealing with."

"A conscientious man."

"I figure you'll be looking at a conscientious judge and prosecutor, too. One thing, at least it isn't an election year. You might end up in TV spots, besides the nightly news. Some dipshit wants to be a senator, describing how he ran you down."

"Your collar, all the way."

"I'm giving it to Elizalde."

"So."

Jack rose and stood before the tinted windows, looking at the bustling streets below.

"These open?"

"No. It's something with the air-conditioning. We're like an airplane here, all sealed and pressurized."

"I never cared for heights, myself."

"I used to know a high-iron worker—Indian, I think he was—who told me all that stuff about not looking down is bullshit. Looking *up* is where you lose it, all that empty sky and nothing solid you can focus on. It blows the mental gyros or something, I don't know."

"At least with looking down, you know how far you've come. How far you have to fall."

"That's just my point. Guy has his head up in the clouds, he doesn't give a shit. Ten feet, ten stories, it's the same. You never really think the ground is down there. Someone's bound to jump in with a safety net if you get that far."

"I don't see any net."

"That's what I get for thinking, eh?"

"You ever see *The Deer Hunter?*"

"Movie with DeNiro? He's in Vietnam?"

"That's it."

"One shot," said Trask.

"You read my mind."

The .38 was nickel-plated, with a two-inch barrel, and as cold as cold could be. If anybody bothered tracing it, the numbers would suggest that it was stolen from a shipment on the New York docks in January 1985.

The weapon left Jack's pocket swaddled in a handkerchief and squeaky clean. One cartridge in the cylinder. He set it on the desk and put the handkerchief away.

"I don't know what I'd do in your position, honestly," he said. "No family to think of. That's a blessing, anyway. You'll take a beating in the media, but that's just words. Stay frosty, keep options open, you might even score a book or movie deal. They have a Son of Sam law here in Texas?"

"I don't know."

"Well, if they do, so what? You sign a deal like Ollie North or Gordon Liddy, give the money to your lawyer or your favorite charity. Some detox center, maybe. A year or two inside, get born again and show up on the 700 Club."

"That movie with DeNiro, how'd it end?"

"Somebody died, I think."

"I guess that's right. They always do."

Jack checked his watch and said, "I'd better get a move on. I'm supposed to call the regional director back and tell him how things stand."

"How do they stand?"

"I haven't made my mind up yet."

"Okay."

He closed the office door behind him, grinning at the startled secretary who hadn't been on duty when he entered, telling her not to worry, they were all friends here.

He was halfway down the corridor, in the direction of the elevators, when he heard a muffled shot. A moment later the secretary came out screaming, giving up her breakfast in a rush.

Clean sweep.

And Fowler had to ask himself the question why it never wound up feeling clean.

EPILOGUE

"Are you all right these days?"

The two of them were outside on Rudy's patio, with beers in hand and burgers on the grill.

"I'm fine."

"It didn't go down quite the way we figured it in Mexico."

"It never does."

They sat and sipped awhile. Stano turned the burgers over, fresh blood hissing on the coals before he said, "The girl helped out a lot, I guess."

"She saved my life a couple of times. No big."

"Reynoso had her locked up in the house, you said. Since she was ten or something?"

"Try fifteen. He called her his fiancée once or twice while I was there. No sign of anybody sending out the wedding invitations that I could see."

"Some deal."

"Some girl. You should've seen her try and take Reynoso's chopper down. I've thought about it, and she probably had no idea he was inside."

"Would it make a difference?"

"Not at all. She was a stand-up lady."

"It's a crying shame we couldn't get her on the payroll, thing like that. She probably would have done all right."

"She *did* just fine."

"That's what I meant to say. You like yours medium?"

"A little on the rare side, if it's not too late."

"By no means. Coming up."

The plates were throwaways, Chinette, with barbecued potato chips and pickles, fresh beers on the side. It smelled delicious. Fowler wished it did not leave a taste of ashes in his mouth.

"Not bad," he managed, after swallowing.

"Not bad? I'll have you know the Stano burger is a living legend, from Palatka to the Keys."

"I stand corrected."

"Now you're talking. Want another?"

"Let me finish one, why don't you?"

"Suit yourself."

They ate in silence for a time, while Rudy worked his way around to business once again. "You need some time?" he asked.

"I'd rather not."

"Because I figure we could swing a couple days if you need to get some rest."

"No point."

"Okay, if you think so."

"Any rumbles from your friend in Dallas?"

"He was satisfied the way it played. They run a standard-issue piece on stress and family problems, this and that. It comes out in the wash."

"I guess."

"Things happen, Jack. You have to let them go."

The bitter taste was back in Fowler's mouth. He washed it down with beer.

"I'm getting pretty good at that, the letting go."

"It's a survival skill, believe me."

"So we're survivors, you and me?"

"We'd better be."

"I guess that's right." Jack smiled, and found it hardly hurt at all. "You want to throw another burger on that grill?"

And Rudy came back at him. "I thought you'd never ask."

**Raw determination in
a stillborn land...**

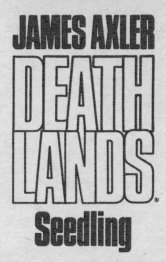

JAMES AXLER

DEATHLANDS®

Seedling

As Ryan Cawdor and his roaming band of survivors desperately seek to escape their nuclear hell, they emerge from a gateway into the ruins of Manhattan.

Under this urban wasteland lives the King of the Underground, presiding over his subterranean fortress filled with pre-nuke memorabilia. And here, in this once-great metropolis, lives Ryan Cawdor's son....

The children shall inherit the earth.

TAKE 'EM NOW

FOLDING SUNGLASSES
FROM GOLD EAGLE

Mean up your act with these tough, street-smart
shades. Practical, too, because they fold 3 times
into a handy, zip-up polyurethane pouch that fits
neatly into your pocket. Rugged metal frame.
Scratch-resistant acrylic lenses. Best of all, they
can be yours for only $6.99.

MAIL YOUR ORDER TODAY.

Send your name, address, and zip code, along with a check or money
order for just $6.99 + .75¢ for delivery (for a total of $7.74) payable to
Gold Eagle Reader Service.
(New York residents please add
applicable sales tax.)

Remove from pouch

unfold once

unfold twice

and they're ready to wear

Gold Eagle Reader Service
3010 Walden Avenue
P.O. Box 1396
Buffalo, N.Y. 14240-1396

GOLD EAGLE

GES-1AR

Offer not available in Canada.

On the savage frontier of tomorrow,
survival is a brand-new game.

SURVIVAL 2000

FROZEN FIRE
James McPhee

David Rand faces his final test—in the third book of Gold Eagle's
SURVIVAL 2000 series.

In the cruel new world created by the devastation of asteroid impacts,
Rand's family is held captive by a murderous gang of army deserters.

With a fortress established in a crumbling mall, the enemy will always
hold the high ground unless Rand can pass the test in a world where
winners die hard . . . and losers live to tell the tale.
